Legacy

A FAMILY OF COURAGEOUS WOMEN

BY ANITA MARTIN-HARVEY

A TRUE LIFE NOVEL

WORD PROJECT PRESS, SONORA

Legacy: A Family of Courageous Women

Published in the United States by
Word Project Press, Sonora, CA

Requests for permission to make copies of any part of this work should be submitted to: harvey1220@comcast.net

Credits:
Photos: Anita Martin-Harvey
Cover Design and Interior Layout:
Melody Young
graphicdesignbymelody.com

ISBN-13: 978-1-7328691-0-3
Second Edition

First Printed 2012
Second Edition Published 2018

Contents

THE NEXT GENERATION

Photos

THIS BOOK IS DEDICATED TO ALL WOMEN EVERYWHERE,
WHO WHEN FACED WITH DISAPPOINTMENT, DIFFICULTY,
AND EVEN DISASTER, FORGE AHEAD AND
NOT ONLY ENDURE, BUT TRIUMPH.

Life is either a daring adventure or nothing.
To keep our faces toward change and behave like free spirits
in the presence of fate is strength undefeatable.
Helen Keller

Courage is not the absence of fear, but rather the judgment that
something else is more important than fear.
Ambrose Redmoon

Success is not measured by what you accomplish, but by the
opposition you have encountered, and the courage with which you have
maintained the struggle against overwhelming odds.
Oscar Sweet Marden

Preface

FAMILY PHOTOS ARE family treasures. They certainly have been in my life. My experience with family photos has been a difficult road at times. At the end of that road I found a surprise and a revelation.

My mother had a lot of photos from her family which I remember seeing when I was very young. There were not only photos of ancestors, but of early California, particularly of Los Angeles and the Hemet-San Jacinto Valley. When my mother died in 1979 at the age of 93, I hoped to have some of these photos. My brother gave most of them to the Hemet Valley Historical Society and others were misplaced. I was disappointed, but several years later, my sister-in-law, Jeanette, found a box of them in her storage shed. I was ecstatic! Here were most of the ancestral pictures I remembered.

My long, painful, marriage ended in 1990 and I moved from the Pacific Northwest to the San Francisco Bay area.. I carefully packed the family photos to take with me. As I settled into my beautiful new place in the Oakland Hills, I framed and hung many of the photos on my living room wall, sorting through those left to possibly put in albums. This was not to be. On a hot, windy Sunday in October 1991, the Oakland Hills Fire swept through my beautiful canyon and destroyed my home. As I ran from the fire for my life, I knew there was no time to rescue the photographs. They were gone.

After my brother died a few years later, his daughter, Julie, started researching the family history. I obtained some copies of a few family pictures from her which I treasured. During her diligent research, Julie found a cousin living in Tracy, California. His name was Jim Bisbee. His grandpa, Chauncey Bisbee, and my Grandma, Emma Bisbee Sexton were brother and sister. Since my husband, Norm, and I live only about sixty miles from Tracy, we called, then made a trip to meet Cousin Jim and his gracious wife, Sylvana.

Jim had just inherited a large box of family photos from his (and my) Uncle Walter Bisbee, the youngest brother of Chauncey and Emma. This was an absolute treasure trove. Jim gave me many original photographs and made copies of others. For Christmas he put together two beautiful scrapbooks of photos, obituaries, cards and other memorabilia and sent them to me. What a miraculous gift!

There were photos of my ancestors that I had never seen before and as I sat and looked at these, I could not believe what I was seeing. Here was Great Grandpa Riley Bisbee when he was a young man and he looks so much like my oldest son, Jeff. Here is Grandma Emma Bisbee Sexton in a young picture, new to me. She looks like my niece, Julie. But the real shocker was a picture of Emma's younger sister, Ada Bisbee when she was twenty-six years old. I hold it in my hand and I am looking at my own face.

So started the urge to tell their stories, to touch on the challenges, the losses, the triumphs, but most of all the emotions of those who came before me. The following is the result of that urge.

—Anita Martin-Harvey

The Beginnings

Sarah Ann Malone, Age 16

SARAH ANN MALONE, AGE 18

INDIANA/OHIO, MID 1800'S

Sarah

WINTER 1843

THE NIGHT VISITORS

SHIVERING, SARAH PULLED the worn quilt tightly around her small, wiry body as she snuggled into her bed. Outside, the wind howled, blowing the snow into drifts against the cabin. The fire still crackled in the fireplace, but somehow the wind inched its icy fingers through tiny cracks between the logs. Da had done a good job with the chinking of the cabin, but the wind had a way of finding the tiniest entrance. Sarah rubbed the soft patchwork against her cheek. She loved this quilt her mother had made from scraps. She would sometimes look at it for hours, searching out remnants from long gone clothing worn by Sarah and her three sisters.

Sarah's sisters were all asleep already. Even Maria, the oldest, was breathing deeply next to her. Sarah felt a welling up of pride knowing she was awake when the others were not.

Well, I am a big girl now, she thought. *I am eight years old, and I can do a lot of big girl things. I can help plant the garden in the spring, weed it in the summer, and bring in the crop. I can feed the chickens and even milk the cow, being careful to strip Daisy's teats, so the milk production does not fall off. I can bring in the wood and make a good fire, and I can even do some of the cooking.*

Sarah counted off her accomplishments and felt proud. Life was not easy here in the Indiana woods for a woman. She was alone most of the time with her four daughters because Da was away working on the new Wabash and Erie Canal. When he did come home, it was time for celebration, as he would bring his pay to give to Ma, not like many of the other Irishmen who drank it all up. Often the family would hitch up the horse, Danny, to the wagon and drive into Fort Wayne or Huntington for supplies. Those days were like a real holiday.

But Da was not here tonight. Maybe that was why Ma had kept the girls up later than usual because she missed him. The venison stew had tasted so good as Ma ladled it into their bowls from the iron pot hanging in the fireplace. The venison came from the deer Da shot on his last trip home. The potatoes, carrots and onions Sarah had helped harvest from the garden were stored for the winter in the small root cellar dug into the earth. These were rationed out carefully so that they would last through the winter. Sarah knew all about how to do this from her mother's careful lessons. Tonight after their supper, Ma pulled out her mending, and the girls gathered around her as she started to tell stories. These could be anything: old legends, fairy tales... or like tonight, memories of her life. Sarah loved these stories the best. She thought her mother was so beautiful with her wavy chestnut hair, clear green eyes, and high cheekbones. Sarah did not think the cluster of wrinkles around her eyes and mouth made her any less beautiful.

Ma's voice was low and musical as she began, "I grew up in the village of Ballinsaloe, called Beal Atha na Slaughe in Gaelic. This was in County Connaught, near Galway. I was thought to be a pretty girl, and my Da was proud of me. Yes, Mary Broderick, was a pretty girl indeed. When I danced to the playing of the fiddles, everyone noticed.

"Indeed, by the time I was sixteen, I had caught the eye of some of the young men in the village, but it was at our annual horse fair that Peter Malone looked at me and liked what he saw. He was much older than I was, but I could not help noticing him with his dark, curly hair and his bright blue eyes. He seemed so much more interesting than the others who were just silly boys.

"By the time I turned seventeen we were seriously courting. We would walk out in the evening and just talk and talk. One night he asked to speak to my Da, and I knew what he would say. He asked my Da for my hand. I was holding my breath, but my Da said 'Yes!' I was so happy for I had come to love Peter Malone with all my heart. Just after I turned eighteen, we were married in the church by our priest, Father Ryan. We started our married life with such hope, but times were hard. Everyone was struggling to put food on the table. Very soon, I realized that we would soon be three and though I was overjoyed upon the prospect of a wee one, I could not help worrying." Ma paused as she seemed to remember this exciting but trying time.

"Some of the young men from the village had left for America. Sometimes they would write letters home, or those who could not write would get someone to write for them. They told of jobs for the many Irish in America. My Peter grew excited with this news. Some had stayed in New York City, but many had gone on to a place called Pittsburgh in Pennsylvania to work in the coal mines. We talked about this between us, your Da, Peter, and me and yes we argued. It would be a hard thing to leave my own Ma and Da here in Ballinsaloe and my brothers and sisters. It would be especially hard now with a little one on the way. Where would the christening be, the family blessing? I could see how determined Peter was to go and how hard I was pulling against this, but one day my sister, Maureen, came to me and said that if we went, she would go with us. That was a turning point for me, and I told Peter I would go. There was no future for us here."

Ma put her mending aside and rose to place more wood on the fire. Sarah could see Maria pull herself up straighter as she soon would be the star of this story. Maria looked so much like Ma with her beautiful hair and striking features. Sarah knew she must look like some other far-off relative with her plain features and mousy brown hair.

"It took many, many weeks to get enough money together to pay for passage on the ship for America. I felt my baby growing within me and knew that I might give birth on the ship in the middle of the Atlantic Ocean. My Peter thought that maybe we should wait until the baby came, but I told him once we had the passage money that we should not wait, but leave for America. And so we did. From bright Galway Bay on a Saturday in May, many days into our voyage—as I knew would happen—my pains began. Maureen helped me, and our beautiful Maria came into this world in the middle of the tossing sea. She was tiny but cried right away, and I knew she would be fine."

Maria squirmed in delight at this part of the story of her birth.

"And so we came to New York. Maureen found work right away as a maid in one of the big homes there, so she decided to stay in this frightening big city. Your Da could not find any work right away, but he heard from Dan Riley from our village that there were jobs in the coal fields near Pittsburgh, so we traveled there with baby Maria, and indeed he did find work, but as the weeks and months went by, I could see how beaten down and discouraged he was becoming. Then one day another friend came by who brought news that many Irish landed jobs working on the new Wabash and Erie Canal. Your Da had carefully saved his wages from the coal company, so taking these, he traveled to Indiana and bought these forty acres in the woods. He came back for us, and we camped in a tent until we built our log cabin. So, my wonderful ones, here we are! To bed with you now, it is way past your bedtime!"

After the girls dived under their covers, Ma came around to hear prayers. She returned to the fireside and her memories. Soon all but Sarah was asleep. Sarah struggled to stay awake. Somehow, she felt this was important. Now she could hear Ma clicking her rosary beads and knew that soon she would bank the fire for the night and take herself to bed. Even in the midst of the blowing winter storm, chores had to be done, and livestock fed early in the morning. All her life, Sarah had heard the night sounds around the cabin. In the summer, the call of night birds and in the winter the howl of the wolf packs that lurked in the woods. These sounds were part of Sarah's life, but tonight there was something different about it. The wolves' howls were louder than usual. There seemed to be more of them and as time passed, the howls came nearer and nearer. Now it sounded as if they were right outside the cabin! It sounded like hundreds of them! Sarah sat up in bed and glanced at the windows in the front wall of the one-room cabin. She gasped, breathless, her heart pounding. There were wolf faces looking right in the window! A lot of wolf faces.

"Ma," she whispered, choking on her words, "Look!" She pointed to the windows. Ma got up slowly from her chair. Taking a dry piece of wood from the pile next to the fireplace, she held it into the fire until the end lit. Raising up this firebrand, she waited to be sure the fire had taken hold, then walked calmly to the door.

By this time, Sarah was standing right behind her in her nightdress, clutching the back of Ma's skirt. Ma reached for the latch. Swinging the door open she faced the raging wolf pack and with a sure arm tossed the burning log into the midst. Snarling, the wolves backed away from the fire, then, one by one, they turned and ran into the woods. Ma quickly slammed and barred the door.

Calmly Ma said, "They were just hungry that's all."

"But," choked Sarah, "they wanted to eat us!"

"Probably. But they won't be back."

It took a long time for Sarah to go to sleep. She had been right to stay awake. Something exciting really did happen, and she was the only one of her sisters to see it.

Sarah

AUTUMN, 1847

THE TOMAHAWK

THE CLEAR BLUE of the sky peeked through the branches of the overhanging trees as Sarah kicked her way through fallen leaves on the forest path. She found herself exulting in an overwhelming sense of well being. October was the most beautiful month in the year for twelve-year-old Sarah. She loved the clarity of the sky, the crispness of the air and the ever-changing beauty of the fall foliage in the woods. It made the long walk home from school more of an adventure than a chore. She walked well ahead of her sisters, Magdalene and Katherine, who answered to Maggie and Katie.

She knew Ma's admonitions to stay together for safety, but Sarah wanted to experience this overwhelming beauty for herself without their incessant chatter. Sarah not only loved the walk to and from school every weekday, but she loved school itself. Learning was exciting, and she could not get enough of it. Her favorite subjects were composition and history. These had come together in the assignment to write about George Washington, the father of their country. Sarah had put a lot of effort into that essay and was rewarded today, by Miss Springfield asking her to read her paper to the class. It didn't matter that her sisters called her "teacher's pet" after school. She knew she had done well and it felt so good.

Ma was fixing the fence when Sarah came into the clearing and as she wielded the hammer called to Sarah.

"I thought I told you to stay with your sisters and here you are way ahead of them. Go change your clothes and clean out the hen-house. It's way overdue."

Oh well, Sarah thought to herself, *Just when I feel so good. The messy clean up of the hen house is the last thing I want to do right now. I would much rather be reading this book I carried home from school.*

But she knew chores were part of life here and they never let up. After changing into her work clothes, Sarah energetically raked the soiled hay from the dirt floor of the hen-house. She heard Maggie's voice raised to a shout.

"Da is coming! Da is coming! I saw him on the hill!"

Any day became a banner day when Da came home for a few days from his work on the Wabash and Erie Canal. Sarah dropped her rake and rushed outside. The three children ran up the hill to meet their father. His wife, Mary, was not far behind. Peter hugged each in turn, then walked with them to the cabin.

"We will have to get word to Maria," Ma exclaimed. Maria had married two years before and lived with her husband in town.

Everyone was excited as they ate their simple meal around the rough-hewn table Da had made. There was much news to catch up on, and the exhilaration continued into the evening. Ma finally sent the girls to bed after each made their last trip to the outhouse. Katie was the last one in and still in a state of excitement unconsciously left the latch string out. She mistakenly thought Maggie was still out there. That would prove to be a glaring mistake.

It took the girls a long time to get to sleep. They were always full of the fun of having Da home for a few days. Mary put out the lamp, and she and Peter undressed and climbed into bed. Sarah had just drifted off when her eyes flew open as she heard the squeak of the front door hinges. Someone was coming into the cabin! In fact, it was a lot of someones. Sarah's heart beat hard in her chest as she counted, one, two, three–there were twelve of them. Sarah shuddered. She knew they were Indians and she did not know what they wanted.

Ma and Da were out of bed now, Da pulling on his britches, Ma throwing a shawl around her shoulders over her flannel nightgown. The Miami Indians lived in the nearby woods in a large village. The settlers and the Indians mostly lived side by side without any hostility, but occasionally there were confrontations. What these twelve wanted was unclear. Soon they formed themselves into a circle in the middle of the small cabin. There were both men and women, dressed in a combination of colorful calico and buckskin. Many of the women carried babies on their backs in shawls or cradle-boards. The group started at once to dance, following each other in the circle. They made only guttural grunts as they navigated the intricate steps, the babies bouncing on their mothers' backs. Peter and Mary turned two chairs around and sat down like royalty being entertained. The three girls stayed in bed and covered their heads with only a tiny hole to peek out at this strange performance. After quite some time, the group stopped dancing, and one by one silently filed out of the cabin.

If the Malones thought that would be the last of their close encounters with the Miamis, they were mistaken. The yearly potato crop was very important to the family. The tubers supplied the major part of their diet during the long winter months. These were dug in the early part of November, piled in a corner of the cabin and later put into the dugout that served as a root cellar. Two days after the night-time visit, Peter came upon several Indians digging up potatoes in the patch behind the cabin. He managed to shoo them off but decided that the family needed to dig up the crop earlier than usual to prevent more raiding of the field. They all pitched in and dug potatoes for the better part of one crisp fall day. Sarah never minded digging potatoes. It was kind of a game, feeling around in the damp earth and coming upon the round, rough skin of another one. The girls made a race of who could find and dig up the most. The potatoes were carried into the cabin and piled in one corner. It looked like a plentiful supply for the coming winter.

Da left to go back to work the next day. Everyone in the family felt sad to see him go. Life was so much easier, and they felt so much safer when he was home, even if only for a few days at a time. They were glad that he had been here to help with the potato stealing problem. They did not know that an even bigger problem would arise about the potatoes. Late one afternoon, a few weeks later, Mary turned from stirring dinner in the pot to see that three Indians had walked into the cabin. At this time of day, the door was almost always unlatched. There were two women and a man. Behind her mother, Sarah stood stock still staring at them. She had no idea what they wanted, and Ma's questioning received no response, although most of the natives understood some English. Silently the trio walked over to the pile of potatoes and using their blankets, started filling them. Sarah was shaking. *What could they do?* Ma was pleading with them to put the potatoes down and just leave, telling them that this was the family's food for the coming winter. They just ignored her pleas. Sarah knew that this was serious. She sensed that Ma was desperate. Seeing the family's food supply disappearing before her eyes, Ma picked up the fireplace tongs and advancing toward the group, started hitting them on their hands and arms.

"Just leave!" she shouted.

Suddenly the man put down his blanket full of potatoes, reached into his clothing and pulled out a tomahawk. Ma was standing next to a small window. As the man started to bring the tomahawk down on Ma, she ducked and grabbed Sarah.

Lifting Sarah's slight body, quickly she shoved her through the open window, shouting, "Go, Sarah, go to the Butler's and get help!"

Shaking, Sarah ran. The George Butler family lived two miles through the woods. Sarah knew the way well, but as she pounded down the trail, careful to not trip over roots and stones, her heart thudded as she kept thinking, *Please God, don't let Ma die. Do something to stop that man from hurting her! Please, please, please!*

Reaching the Butler cabin, she immediately saw George working outside. Running up to him and gasping for breath, she choked, "Please come help us! The Indians are in our cabin, and one is trying to kill Ma!"

George put the bridle on his horse, Lucy, and pulling Sarah up with him, mounted and whipped Lucy into a gallop. Sarah held on for dear life and kept praying, trying not to see her mother dead and bleeding on the floor. When they arrived, both dashed into the cabin and found Ma sitting on a chair, her face pale and drawn, but unhurt.

"I think putting you out the window to go for help scared them off Ma gasped.

"They didn't have any guns, and they didn't know how far away the Butlers lived." Sarah threw her arms around her mother.

"Ma, I thought I would find you dead!" Tears filled her eyes and ran down her cheeks. Ma patted her gently on the back.

"No, my babe, I am still here. And you, my little one, were very brave indeed to have run so far for your poor Ma."

SPRING 1850

THE ACCIDENT

THE CABIN DOOR squeaked as Mary pushed it open. A warm breeze ruffled her hair. She breathed deeply and let her senses absorb the bright green beauty of an Indiana Spring day. It reminded her of springtime in Ireland so many years ago. Her thoughts flew back to that time when she went walking with Peter near Ballinsaloe. She remembered how it felt for it to be Spring and in love. A beautiful ballad from those days leapt into her mind, and she could not keep still:

> The moon was bright
> The night was clear.
> No breeze came over the sea.
> When Mary left her Highland home
> And wandered forth with me
> The flowers be-decked the mountainside
> And fragrance filled the vale
> But by far the sweetest flower there
> Was the rose of Allendale

Oh the rose of Allendale Sweet rose of Allendale
By far the sweetest flower there
Was the rose of Allendale

Mary's voice, clear and sure, sailed up into the pine trees in the nearby woods. *Enough of this silliness,* she thought. This won't get the chores done! High on the list today was to pen up Buttercup, Daisy's calf. Mary smiled to herself. The children had named the newest female offspring and showered a lot of loving attention on her. However, Buttercup was able to drink out of a bucket now and needed to be weaned from her mother. Another smile flitted across Mary's face at her recollection of dipping her fingers into the milk in the bucket, allowing Buttercup to suck from her fingers until she could lap up the milk without encouragement. It was time to move on. Buttercup would eventually be sold to become someone else's milk cow. Daisy's milk could then be turned into butter and cheese which would be sold to neighbors. Money was tight, and a strict schedule had to be kept.

Mary dreaded this chore, however, because both Buttercup and Daisy would protest the separation. The sorrowful bellowing would continue for several days and yes, even through the nights. As Mary passed the garden plot, she paused to view the progress of the sprouting plants. They were coming along nicely, but so were weeds. Glad for an excuse, she knelt at the edge of the plot and pulled several, tossing them aside. She kept at this for some time, singing again:

"Where e'er I wandered east or west,
Though fate began to lour,
A solace still was she to me
In sorrow's lonely hour.
When tempests lashed our lonely barque
And rent her quivering sail
One maiden's form withstood the storm

'Twas the rose of Allendale.
Oh sweet rose of Allendale,
Sweet rose of Allendale,
One maiden's form withstood the storm,
'Twas the rose of Alloendale."

At last, Mary stood and brushed off her hands. The main job of the day had to be done. She could put it off no longer. Picking up a short rope, she unfastened the gate to the cow pen. Walking up to Buttercup, she looped the rope around her neck. Daisy, sensing something unusual happening lowed deeply. Mary tugged gently on the rope urging Buttercup toward the gate. This seemed to alarm Daisy even more. Daisy suddenly stepped sideways launching her formidable flank into Mary. Mary dropped the rope and stepped backward, but tripped and lost her balance. Suddenly she found herself landing on top of a fence post. A searing pain ripped through her, taking her breath away. She slid to the muddy ground clutching her side. Waves of pain overwhelmed her.

Mary lay there panting for what seemed like an eternity. Gradually, she was able to pull herself upright, open the gate and sinking to her knees, crawled through. Gasping with the excruciating pain, Mary managed to inch her way slowly toward the cabin. She collapsed on the steps, and everything went black. The hours crawled by. She would briefly regain consciousness, gasp and moan with the pain, and then black out again. When would the children be home from school? It seemed to take forever.

The three sisters walked home through the woods, unaware of their mother's plight. For a time Sarah joined in with Maggie and Katie's chatter but soon retreated as usual to her own thoughts. Fifteen now, she had two more years at the country school. Just this day Miss Springfield had taken her aside and surprised her with something both exciting and amazing. As usual, she praised Sarah's hunger for learning, telling her she was perhaps her very best student ever.

Then she said, "Sarah, I am getting older, and eventually I want to move to Ohio to be near my brother and his family. I would like to do that two years from now because I believe that when you graduate, you could take over my position as the schoolmistress. Would you consider doing this?"

Sarah did not have to think twice, "Oh yes, Miss Springfield, I would love to do that!"

"Good, good, I am so happy that you would consider this."

Sarah could not help dreaming about this wonderful turn of events as she walked home.

Thoughts flew from her mind as she approached the cabin. *What in the world? Is that Ma lying on the steps? Something is very wrong.* She started running. Maggie and Katie, sensing Sarah's alarm started running too.

"Ma, Ma, what's wrong?" Sarah shouted. Mary did not respond. "She's hurt! Help me carry her inside," she begged her sisters.

Gently grasping her shoulders and legs, the girls carried her into the cabin and laid her on her bed. Her thin frame made Sarah realize just how much her mother had changed.

"She's hurt bad!" Sarah turned to Maggi, "Run to the Butlers!" she gasped. "Get Mr. Butler to ride into town and fetch the doctor!"

Maggie immediately sprinted out the door. Sarah turned to her mother who was again conscious and moaning with pain. Sarah wet a cloth with cold water and laid it gently on her forehead. Mary's face now had a gray cast to it, and her breathing was labored. Sarah was scared. The thought rushed in that maybe her Ma was dying. *No, no, this can't be! I can't lose her! Please, dear God, save her life. You answered my prayer once before when I thought the Indian might kill her with the tomahawk. Please, please, save her again!"*

It seemed forever when the cabin door flew open and Mr. Butler, Maggie, and Dr. Knowles stumbled in. The doctor immediately knelt down by the bed and took Mary's hand, feeling for her pulse. He then took out his stethoscope. Putting the small end to his ear, he laid the horn-like end on her chest and listened to her heart and lungs.

Looking up, he said, "I'm sorry, but your mother has been gravely injured. I believe she has fractured a rib and that has punctured her lung. I do not think I can save her."

"No, no!" Sarah cried. She choked off a sob. Mr. Butler patted Sarah on the shoulder.

"I am so sorry," he said in a quiet voice. "I know that you Catholics believe in having a priest anoint you and forgive your sins when you are dying. I didn't think it looked good for Mrs. Malone here, so I stopped by the Catholic church and asked Father Reilly to come out with us. He had a meeting going and said he couldn't get away, but he would come later."

Anger flared up in Sarah's chest. *Could not get away? Her mother was going to die, and she knew the priest would not get here in time. Was it because the Malones only attended confession and Mass sporadically? Or was it because it took all their resources just to survive and did not put money in the church coffers?* Sarah's thoughts were in turmoil.

Dusk darkened the cabin. Mary's breathing had become gasps for air. All color had drained from her face. She was barely conscious, but her thoughts were focused.

"Peter!" she gasped.

"Oh no," Sarah whispered. In all of this, she had almost forgotten about Da. Of course, he should be here and right now.

Mr. Butler again laid his hand on Sarah's shoulder. "It's taken care of. I sent for your father up to the canal works. I am sure he will be here just as soon as he can."

Sarah breathed out in relief.

Mary's eyes were wide open and staring now. Peter! She saw him as he was so long ago in County Connaught, dark hair covering his brow, as he came walking over the hill. Strangely, the song she had sung early that day came back to her in her mind:

The moon was bright, the night was clear
No breeze came over the sea.
When Mary left her Highland home
And wandered forth ....

As they all watched, the life left Mary's eyes. She was gone. Maggie and Katie started sobbing hysterically. Sarah clamped her jaw shut and choked down a scream. God had not heard her, had not answered her prayer this time. The doctor expressed his condolences. Mr. Butler left with him, saying on his way out, "Please let me know if I can do anything. I'll send Mrs. Butler over to help out."

Eventually, Sarah arose and calling her sisters, set about washing her mother's body and dressing her in her best dress. She gently combed her mother's hair, noticing how grey it had turned. Mary was forty-five years old. When the dawn broke over the forest, Sarah realized that the priest had never come as promised. Her mother lay there unshriven. In no way would she believe that her soul had gone to Hell because of this.

By mid-morning, her Da arrived. Walking into the cabin, he choked as he saw Mary laid out on the bed with her hands crossed on her chest. He knelt by her side and took her in his arms and cried silently for a long time. Finally rising to his feet, Da gathered his daughters to him and held them as they all cried together. Soon, he left to go to town. He would bring the sad news to Maria, now living there with her new Irish husband, James O'Hara. He would also buy some pine boards to build a coffin. Later they could hear the pounding of the hammer as he fashioned it.

Numbly, Sarah watched her father climb the nearby hill with his shovel and start digging. When he was finished, he came back inside and asked the girls to help him lift their mother into the pine box and together carry her up the hill. Sarah did not ask why Ma was being buried here instead of in consecrated ground at the Catholic cemetery. Not only would the awful Father Reilly not have allowed it, but they also did not have the money for it. After a hymn and a short prayer, Peter shoveled dirt onto the coffin. The next several days Peter was gone a lot into town. He did not tell the girls what he was doing, but Sarah somehow knew it involved their future as a family. The girls kept things together and Mrs. Butler came in to help, but they were barely aware of their surroundings as they took turns cooking and doing the chores. Finally, at the end of the week Peter gathered them all together.

"I have made plans for you," he said solemnly. "You may not like them, but it is the best that I can do. I cannot keep the farm. I still have my job to do, and I cannot expect three young girls to run this alone. Jed Michaels up the road has offered to buy the forty acres and the cabin. He plans for his son-in-law to run the place. I have found a position for Katie at the Nerdlingers in Fort Wayne. She will be caring for their children. Maggie will go to live with Maria and James. Sarah, you will go to the Jewish tailor, Isaac Hirsch, where Maria did the apprenticeship. He and his wife will be kind to you as they were to Maria and he will teach you the tailoring business. Now, any questions?"

Maggie and Katie were brimming with questions. They seemed excited and saw this as a new adventure.

Sarah was speechless. *What about school? What about Miss Springfield's offer of the teaching position in two years? This was not going to happen.* Sarah finally found her voice. "Can't I find a place at the Nerdlingers too, so I could be with Katie."

"No," Peter replied. "That is not possible, Sarah. I will talk to you alone later."

As promised, Da pulled her aside sometime later. Looking at her solemnly, he pronounced, "Sarah, you are the smartest of all my children. That is why I want you to go to the Hirsch's for training in a trade. Maria is already married. Maggie and Katie are pretty enough to find a suitable husband. Unfortunately, you are plain, Sarah. But you are smart, and if you do not find a husband, at least you will have the skills to support yourself."

With that he turned and walked away leaving Sarah to think. *I have lost everything: my home, my family, my education, my future. And on top of that, my father thinks I am ugly!*

JANUARY

THE TAILOR SHOP

SARAH BENT HER thin frame over the cutting table. Her shiny shears slid through the heavy wool serge like butter. The dark blue color pleased her. This would become a handsome coat for Mr. Robert Forester, a prosperous merchant here in Fort Wayne. The Hirsch tailor shop was always busy. Isaac Hirsch was known for his quality work and fair prices. Sarah felt a sense of pride that she was now able to put together a garment from start to finish and skillfully at that.

Sarah smiled to herself as she remembered the day she had arrived in this household. The day after her Da told her that this would be her new home, she packed up her meager belongings and rode with Da into Fort Wayne. Sarah was silent on the trip, sitting stiffly on the wagon seat.

Isaac Hirsch answered her Da's knock,

"Here she is," her Da stated in a matter of fact manner.

Sarah thought bitterly, *I feel like a package being delivered.* Isaac Hirsch fastened his piercing gaze on her.

"Gants gut—*Very good.* Today you feel you do not have a briere—*a choice*, but kein briere iz ouch a briere—*not to have a choice is a choice.*"

Sarah thought, *What a crazy old man. Now, over two years later, she would say, What a wise old man!*

Sarah had arrived in the Hirsch household silent, angry and rebellious. Her world had shattered, and she just wanted to lash out. She was angry at God for not hearing her desperate plea. She was angry at Father Reilly for ignoring her mother's pli, ht and as a result, she was very angry at the whole Catholic church. She was angry at Da for making this choice for her, and yes, even angry at Ma for leaving them. She had made the decision that in no way would she like it here, would just endure until she could get away.

Sarah again smiled. She was certainly no longer that hostile, furious, fifteen-year-old. What had changed her? The love and acceptance of the entire Hirsch family.

Isaac was a thin, stooped man with frizzy hair and an equally frizzy graying beard. Miryam was his total opposite, round and soft like the dumplings she loved to make. Her pink cheeks almost always crinkled in a smile. She wore a head scarf and an apron and loved to hug. That first day she gathered Sarah up in her embrace and Sarah stiffened in resistance, but Miryam was not discouraged. The hugs continued. Miryam also lavished hugs on her two boys, Moses, called Moishe, ten and Samuel, Shmueli, eight, The Hirsches were quite a bit older than Ma and Da. They had married late. Sarah came to love the boys deeply, enjoying having little brothers for a change.

The small tailor shop was on the main floor and opened onto the street. The family lived two floors above the shop. The rooms were comfortable and immaculately kept. Sarah was shown to her room that first day and could not help but be in awe of where she was to live. The room was small, but had asingle bed with a beautifully crafted quilt covering it. It also had a rocking chair of burnished wood, a dresser with a washbasin and pitcher on it and a small desk with a lamp. Used to the shared beds in the one-room cabin she had called home, this was luxury beyond her wildest dreams. She stilled her beating heart and reminded herself that this would not change her refusal to enjoy this sojourn. Sarah remembered her first meal in the household. Somehow, she had pictured herself eating alone in the kitchen, excluded from the family, as the hired help she felt herself to be. She was surprised when Miryam took her by the hand and led her to the table to sit between Moishe and Shmueli who both acted silly, vying for her attention. A further surprise was the very strange, but delicious food that Miryam had prepared. After prayer, Isaac said.

"Ess gezunterheit!–*eat in good health*" Thus, started what would turn out to be her first lesson in Yiddish. Pointing to each dish in turn, Isaac named it then translated.

"Hendl mit knaidell–*chicken and dumplings,* shav–*cold spinach soup,* holishkess–*stuffed cabbage,* glezel taii–*glass of tea.* Later we have kugel–*pudding."*

Sarah had thought to refuse to eat in protest of her situation, but she was so hungry and the smells , tantalized her. When Miryam handed her a well-filled plate, she dove in and ate every bite. Looking at Miryam, Isaac exclaimed.

"Tsegit zich in moy!–*It melts in your mouth."*

"Me ken lecken di finger!–*It is delicious!"*

Sarah would soon find that Isaac was generous in his praise of Miryam. How many times had she heard him exclaim, "She is some balebooteh!" in praise of her housekeeping skills.

The very next day after her reluctant arrival, Isaac set out to teach her the tailoring trade. Sarah had learned to sew simple garments and had helped her mother piece together quilts, but fashioning suits and coats and similar garments was a whole new world. Isaac was a patient and persistent teacher.

He would lace his instructions with sayings in Yiddish, from admonitions such as:

"A foiler tut in tsveyenn–*A lazy person has to do a task twice to deserved praise."*

"A leben ahfdein kepel–*A life on your head!*" Meaning you are so smart!

With the warmth and acceptance of the family and the knowledge and praise she received, Sarah slowly began to thrive. She ate well, she slept well, and she enjoyed creating the garments in the shop. With Isaac's patient translation of Yiddish, she soon became able to communicate in the language, eventually becoming fluent.

Sarah's anger and disappointment at having to leave school was assuaged by the discovery that the Hirsches had an extensive library. It seemed that Isaac was quite a scholar. Many of the books were in Hebrew and though Sa, ah tried to master the strange alphabet and words, it was slow going. However, the library also contained wonderful volumes in English. She loved the literature and read Shakespeare, Dante's *Divine Comedy* and other books avidly, but her real joy was the books on world and ancient history, especially archaeology. Isaac gave her permission to take books to her room at night where she poured over them by the warm glow of the lamp on her desk.

Early in her stay at the Hirsch's Sarah would see Maria, Maggie and Katie often. Maria's husband, James O'Hara, had answered the call of the gold-fields and gone by wagon train to San Francisco, a trip that took him six months. He quickly established a business selling picks and shovels to the miners and after a year sent for Maria and Maggie and the two small O'Hara children. The sisters traveled to California by way of Panama and their letters to Sarah described a harrowing ordeal. Sarah missed them so very much. She seldom saw Da. She felt he had betrayed her mother and her memory when he remarried two years ago, a German woman he had met in Fort Wayne. They had a child now, Peter, named after Da. Sarah guessed he was very happy to have a son after four girls. The construction on the canal had been completed for some time, but Peter had taken a job on the canal barges. Work was plentiful as so many of the canal laborers had left to rush to California to dig for gold. Sarah had been aware of the discovery of gold at Sutter's Mill in northern California in 1848, but it wasn't until Maria's husband, was bitten by the "gold bug," that this event hit home. Sarah wrote to her sisters in California often and told them the news of her life and Katie's.

In the over two years with the Hirsch family, Sarah had still not sorted through her confusion over her faith. She moved away from her anger at God for taking her mother, instead, castigating herself for not having enough faith. She lost her anger at Father Reilly. She had not attended confession or Mass since coming to Fort Wayne. Sometimes she felt that she was hovering in that existence Catholics believed to be the place of unbaptized babies, Limbo. But she was no baby. She was an intelligent young adult and ought to be able to sort out what she believed.

Sarah came to love the special meal on *Shabbat Eve*. It would start with the sound of a metal cup banging against the shutters of the tailor shop as the *Shabbat Klopper* notified the Jewish neighborhood that sundown was approaching. Sarah and Isaac would lay aside their work and climb the stairs. The table would be ready, together with the two candles to be lit by Miryam. As she performed this task, she would sing a lovely Hebrew song slightly off key. *Kiddish*, a blessing, would be said over the wine and *Kaddish*, the prayer for dead friends and family members. The meal was always special, Miryam having spent hours in the kitchen preparing it.

For a long time, Sarah had politely refused to accompany the family to the *Shabbat* service after the meal at the nearby *Shul*. Having heard all her life that entering any church, but a Catholic one would result in her eternal damnation, she still held some fear in her heart. She would also sometimes remember Father Reilly saying from his pulpit that all Jews were "Christ killers," but as she was folded into the love of this family, this thought seldom entered her mind.

Of course Father Reilly would never have come calling at a Jewish home, but one day as Sarah was running an errand for Isaac, she came face to face with the cleric.

"Sarah!" he exclaimed, "How good to see you. I have missed you at church. Do remember, dear Sarah, that you have to come to confession and receive the Eucharist or you risk eternal damnation." His smile was insincere.

Sarah did not respond, but turned her back on the odious priest and marched back to the shop. "Showngenug!–*That's enough!* Adeigeh hob ich!–*I don't care!*" she muttered.

She was surprised how easily the Yiddish words sprang to her tongue. *The Jews really know how to express their feelings,* she thought.

The encounter with Father Reilly was a turning point. At the next Shabbat Eve dinner, Sarah told Isaac and Miryam that she would accompany them to the service at the *Shul.* The Hirsches looked surprised but pleased and they all walked the short distance to the *Shul* together. As they approached, Sarah saw women with their heads covered together with their children, men with their shoulders covered with a *talliss* or prayer shawl, the skullcaps or *yarmulkes* on their heads. When they entered, the women and children filed to one side, the men to the other. A rough curtain separated them. The reading was from the *Shul's* special *Torah,* then prayers, after which everyone moved into an adjoining room for a get together called *Oneg Shabbatt.* Coffee and tea were served along with *Schnecken,* little fruit and nut coffee rolls. Everyone was chattering at once and Sarah tried to translate all of the Yiddish she was hearing, but it was impossible. She sensed the warmth of the people and felt at home here as in the Hirsch's home. Would she become Jewish? She did not think so, but this indeed was special. These people lived their beliefs.

Sarah had changed too in the matter of her appearance. Cut by Da's assessment of her as "plain," Sarah had soon after that sought out a mirror and studied her likeness. She saw a thin, drawn face topped by mousy brown hair. She had to agree with Da. There was only one small mirror in the log cabin and she had hardly ever looked at herself in it. Now, she was surrounded by mirrors, especially in the tailor shop where fittings were a continual way of life. At first, she would look away as she passed them, but gradually she sneaked a peek. As she viewed her face as well as her slender form in its entirety, she could see herself gradually changing. She filled out some and her face lost its sourness. While she knew she would never be a beauty, she came to see herself as attractive enough.

The Hirsch's esteem certainly built up her confidence. On her sixteenth birthday, they surprised her with a beautiful new dress of bronze silk. It had been a joint effort: Isaac fashioning the pattern and basic sewing and Miryam sewing the many rows of ruching. It fit perfectly and the family then marched her to the photography studio for her portrait. This photo and the dress were now Sarah's most prized possessions.

Sarah had let her mind wander, but her hands kept busy at her task. It was second nature now to skillfully cut and fashion a garment. She was startled back to the present as she listened to loud voices from the front of the shop. A customer had come in. It was a Jewish acquaintance of Isaac's.

"Vi gail dos gesheff?–*How's business?*" the customer inquired.

"Ei, ei oysgemutshett!–*Oh! Oh! I am worked to death!*" Saul Birnbaum proceeded to inquire about a topcoat for himself.

"Vifil?–*How much?*"

Isaac quoted a price, some haggling took place. Finally, settling on a price, Isaac quipped, "Gelt oyfrn tish!–*Don't ask for credit!*"

Saul laughed, "A klog iz mir!–*Woe is me!*" Turning, he opened the door and left, calling over his shoulder, "Le chayim!"

The shneider (*the tailor*) chortled, "Ot azaih–*That's how, just like that!*"

Sarah loved the interplay between Isaac and his customers. She heard the door open again. Well, perhaps there will be more entertainment. However, it was the postman with a handful of letters. Isaac took them and sorting through them, called to Sarah. There is one here for you, from California.

"Oh good," Sarah said. "It will be from Maria."

But the writing on the envelope was not Maria's. Curious, she slit open the envelope. Two pieces of paper fell out. One was a short letter. She picked it up and started to read:

Dear Sarah,

I am sorry to have to write you with some bad news. Maria is very ill. As you know from her, she has suffered several miscarriages. These have worn her down and now the doctor says she has consumption. She is no longer able to do the housework for us and I am trying hard to keep her in bed to get rest as well as keep the household going. She keeps asking for you, hoping that you might make your way to California to care for her. I do beg you to consider this, as it would mean so much to her. I am enclosing a cheque for your fare. I regret it is not more, but it is all I can afford. If you do come, the Panama route is the quickest. I do hope and pray you can see your way clear to come and comfort your sister.

Affectionately yours,

Your brother-in-law,

James O'Hara

Sarah sat in stunned silence Isaac walked up behind her. "Vos iz?– *What's the matter?*"

Sarah handed him the letter to read. "Nisht fur dich gedacht"– *This shouldn't happen.*"

Turning, Sarah looked into Isaac's kind and wise face, "What shall I do? I am so happy here and I know you told me I might be good enough to open up my own shop? California? It is so far away and I would have to go alone."

"A mentsh tracht und Gott lacht,–*A person plans and God laughs,*" Isaac sighed. "I know you are a shikseh, but you are so much more than just a boarderkeh,–*a female boarder,* you are like a tochter–*A daughter* and Miryam and I are your mameh and tateh. Gloib mirr! Ich hob dir lieb–*Believe me, I love you!*"

"Ich vais–*I know,*" Sarah sighed. "I am hartsvalik und verklempt – *heartsick and on the verge of tears.*" Isaac patted her shoulder. Sarah suddenly felt incredibly ongematert–*tired.* Picking up her letter and the cheque, she slowly stumbled up the stairs to her room.

When Sarah finally wandered down to dinner, Miryam gathered her up in her arms. "My kinderlech–*I am so sorry.*"

Sarah leaned into her. It felt like being enveloped in a soft down comforter, making Sarah wish she could only stay there forever. "It is so hard, but I believe that I have to go to my sister. We were so close growing up. She was older, so she always looked out for me. Now it is my turn."

Tears brimmed in Miryam's eyes. "Ir gefelt mir zaierr–*You please me very much.*"

After dinner, Isaac sat down with Sarah. "How much did your brother-in-law send you to pay for the trip?" When Sarah told him, Isaac replied. "I do not believe that is nearly enough. I will help with the money."

When Sarah protested, Isaac pronounced, "Gelt is nist kayn dayge. –*Money is not a problem.* I will also give you the name and address of an old friend of mine, Elias Goldman, who has a tailor shop in San Francisco. He will give you a place to stay when you arrive and work if you need it. I will write a letter of introduction and I will recommend you highly."

"Thank you so much. You are so kind. I do not feel I deserve all this." Sarah returned.

"Remember, you are a kemfer and a alrightnikey–*a fighter and a woman who succeeds,* and you are my tochter." He lovingly patted her hand.

Soon Moishe and Shmueli were jumping up and down around her, singing, "Sarah's going on a trip, Sarah's going on a trip. A long, long way. All the way to Californ-ee-ay."

Sarah had to laugh then. She tousled their hair and pulled them to her, her adorable little brothers.

The next day, Sarah posted a letter to Maria and her husband and packed her things in a tapestry bag that Miryam gave her, giving special care to the birthday dress and the portrait. Isaac pressed a volume of Plutarch's writings into her hands.

She held it close to her, "I will treasure this and all my memories of all of you."

Finally, they were ready and the whole family walked Sarah to the station where she would catch the stagecoach for New York City. As she was ready to board, she turned and gave each one a hug.

Isaac, wiped his eyes and said, "Vahksin zuls du tsu gezunt, tsu leven, tsu langehyor.—*May you grow to health, to life, to long years.*"

Sarah choked back a sob and replied, "Vus du vinsht mir, vensh ikh dir.—*What you wish me, I wish you.*"

She climbed up into stagecoach, her heartbreaking once again. As the stagecoach pulled away, she did not look back.

EIGHTEEN YEARS EARLIER

HAMILTON COUNTY, OHIO, NEAR CINCINNATI,
ONE-HUNDRED-FIFTY MILES
FROM THE CABIN IN THE INDIANA WOODS

Ann

1835

A Quaker Wedding

THE SOFTLY ROLLING hills of Hamilton County were bright green with sprouting Spring grass. Nestled among the hills, the Ohio River flowed relentlessly on, wending into Indiana, eventually to find its way to the mighty Mississippi and the sea. Golden sunlight tumbled through lace-curtained windows and pooled on the polished pine floor of the comfortable Claypoole home. Eighteen-year-old Ann Claypoole basked in its warmth. Clear ivory skin, light brown hair pulled into a bun beneath her Quaker bonnet and clear blue eyes gave her a pleasing countenance. A comforting warmth spread through her body, not from the sunshine, but from Ann's thoughts of her upcoming marriage to the handsome Richard Kinnan Sexton.

Not letting her thoughts slow her down in her task, Ann's fingers flew as she sewed tiny stitches into the tucks on her white linen petticoat. No one at the simple wedding ceremony would see her petticoat, of course, but she would know it was there under her plain grey dress. Sometimes Ann allowed herself to wish that she could wear a beautiful white dress and veil, have brightly clad bridesmaids and even a flower girl at her wedding as some of her schoolmates had done. However, that was impossible as Ann's family belonged to the Society of Friends. They were Quakers.

Ann's family could trace their Quaker history back to its founder, George Fox, in seventeenth-century England. Fox's quest to find a simpler, more meaningful Christianity had led to his being imprisoned four times, beaten and tortured unmercifully for his beliefs. Many of his followers met the same fate, so it was natural that these believers found a refuge in America. Ann's ancestor, James Claypoole, was a close friend of William Penn and traveled with him to the New World to found the colony of Pennsylvania.

Ann was taught to be proud of her family and their accomplishments. James Claypoole was not the first dissenter. A Claypoole married the favorite daughter of Oliver Cromwell, while other parts of that family remained royalists, loyal to Charles I. A Claypoole married Betsy Ross, the legendary maker of the American flag. Further back were even grander ancestors.

Ann was born in Pennsylvania to Joseph and Anne Woodhouse Claypoole. When she was very small, the family moved to New Jersey. She did not remember that event at all. When it was time to start school, she attended a Quaker school there. She was twelve when her parents decided to move to the far west and set out for Hamilton County in Ohio. Ohio was the frontier, and the move was a distressing event for Ann. Leaving her little school and her friends and relatives was very difficult. Once settled in Ohio, Ann enrolled in the school in their community which was not Quaker. It was a hard adjustment for her. She did well in her studies, but she looked forward to being finished.

This was helped along by her budding romance with Richard Sexton made the adjustment a bit easier. Four years older than Ann, she had noticed him from the beginning when he came by the school to pick up his younger brother and sister, Ezekiel and Mary, in his carriage. His erect bearing, broad smile and outgoing personality made him stand out.

There were other occasional encounters in town, and Ann was sure that Richard noticed her also. Soon, they began to converse, and Ann discovered Richard possessed a flair and love of life that she found very attractive. He had a wonderful sense of humor. His personality was a contrast to Ann's quiet, proper ways. He challenged her, and this drew her to him even more strongly.

Richard's family was almost as distinguished as the Claypooles. A Sexton had immigrated to America at about the same time as the first Claypoole. George Sexton had come to Windsor, Connecticut in 1663. The family was Anglo Irish and had many distinguished antecedents as did the Claypoole's. One of Richard and Ann's favorite games was to try to prove which of their ancestors were more important.

Ann would chide, "Thou knows that my great, great, great, whatever grandfather was the mayor of Culross in Scotland and a Member of Parliament!"

"That's nothing," Richard would laugh. "My great, great, great, whatever grandfather was four times the mayor of Limerick in Ireland and besides married the former mayor's daughter!"

Chastened, Ann would bristle, "I had many, many Sir Knights in my family, so there!"

"Well, I did too, and besides that, one of my great, greats served in the Court of Henry VIII." Richard would respond.

"Served a king, huh. My ancestor was a king. King Edward I, so there!"

By this time Ann's voice would have risen an octave and squeaked with emotion. At this point, they would both double over in laughter until tears surfaced.

Ann came to love Richard's quick thinking, his curiosity, and his ambition. She soon decided after getting to know him that she wanted to marry him and spend the rest of her life with him. When it became apparent that they were becoming serious about each other, both families expressed some concern. While Ann's parents had responded early to Richard's natural charm, they worried that he was not a Quaker. Richards's family hesitated for the same reason. They were Baptists. The Sextons from the time of Henry VIII had been Anglicans in England and Ireland. However, a Sexton ancestor, Daniel, and his wife, Sarah, became members of a Baptist Church in Middletown, New Jersey. They apparently grew dissatisfied with this church and took their membership to Crosswicks Baptist Church where they stayed seven years. That did not last either, so they then started their own church: Jacobstown Baptist in 1785 with thirty-two members. The family had been Baptists ever since.

Ann, used to the "silent meetings" of the Society of Friends, found Baptist services upsetting with the loud, "Hallelujahs, Praise the Lords!" and "Amens. Both Ann's and Richard's fathers entered one time into a heated debate over the Bible and its place in a Christian's life. Richard's father held that the Bible was God's Word and the last authority in the life of a believer. Joseph Claypoole, however, according to his Quaker belief, held that while the Bible did come from God, it was not the end all authority in life. That was the "inner voice of the Spirit." He quoted a noted Quaker writer, Robert Barclay, who in his *Apology*, written in 1678 said, "[the Scriptures] are only a declaration of the fountain, and not the fountain itself, therefore they are not to be esteemed the principal ground of all truth and knowledge, nor yet the adequate primary rule of faith and manners."

Daniel Sexton, pounded the table, shouting, "It's the Bible! God's holy word. This is what I believe!" Somehow, the two managed to mend their theological differences, perhaps because Richard found the quiet of the Friends' meetings he attended with Ann more to his liking and the elder Sextons. Seeing his commitment to her, their fathers gave in and gave their blessing to the upcoming marriage. Richard felt the four "Testimonies" of the Quakers expressed a noble goal. Peace, Equality,

Integrity (Truth) and Simplicity.

The plans for the wedding then proceeded without further contention. According to Quaker custom, Richard and Ann wrote a letter to the clerk of the meeting indicating their intention to wed. The meeting found no objection to their marriage and three persons were appointed to assist the couple in planning the event. These three, two men and a woman saw to the wording of the marriage certificate, signed it at the time of the marriage, and would oversee a simple reception following. A date was set, and members of the meeting notified of the event.

Ann's fingers flew as she completed her task on the petticoat. Now it was only two days to the big event. All of Ann's dreams for her life were unfolding before her eyes. She almost pinched herself to be sure it was really happening. Mama Anne had trained both Ann and her sisters in household tasks. Ann was able to cook a delicious meal with many tasty dishes and serve it graciously using the silver and Spode china. Ann would receive her own set of china for a wedding gift from her parents. She knew how to fold the soft linen napkins, placing them to the left on the tablecloth. Ann had spent hours hemming an equally lovely cloth and matching napkins for her bride's chest. Ann's dream was to marry someone she loved, to live in a lovely home as gracious as the one she had grown up in and to have many beautiful children. both boys and girls, a family like her own with her nine brothers and sisters. She could see herself living her life in this beautiful setting, growing old together with her husband.

One day, a few weeks before, the senior Sextons invited Ann and Richard to dinner. After the meal, they sat together as Richard's father cleared his throat and spoke, "I have decided to deed this farmhouse and land to you two for a wedding gift. We will be moving to our other smaller place down the road. The place is too much work at our age, and it will be good for you and your growing family to live in this big house. Farming the land is much too taxing for me now, but you and

Richard are young and strong. I am pleased to do this!"

Ann could hardly believe it. The large, gracious farmhouse built in the 1700's would now be their home. She could hardly wait, not only to become Richard's wife, but to move into the beautiful home where she would spend the rest of her life.

On the appointed day, as Ann awoke, her eyes flew open, and she sang out, "This is my wedding day."

As she carefully bathed her lithe body, she thought, *I do hope Richard will be pleased with me in every way.*

After a simple breakfast that she hardly touched, Ann climbed up to her bedroom to dress. Slipping the linen petticoat over her head, she paused to admire the rows of tiny tucks. *I did an excellent job on this,* she thought. Next came the soft grey dress with the white collar.

Her mother came into her room and paused to look at her. "Thou look lovely, daughter. So happy, and I am happy for thee. Mama moved over to Ann and gave her a gentle hug. "Now sit down, so I can do thou hair. Ann complied, and her mama brushed her light brown hair until it shone, then deftly twisted it into a bun low on her neck. She then placed the grey bonnet on Ann's head. "There, all ready for thou big moment!"

There was a parade of Claypooles wending their way to the meeting house on the day of the wedding. Her married brothers, William and George, and their families came in their own conveyances. Her next older sibling, Joseph, drove the wagon carrying her sisters, Hannah, Rebecca, Harriet Matilda, Mary, Jane, and Elizabeth. Mama, Papa and Ann rode separately in the carriage. It was so wonderful to have her whole large family here for her great day. Ann's heart seemed to beat right out of her chest as she was so excited. Richard and his family arrived at about the same time. Quakers did not observe the taboo of the groom not seeing the bride before she marched down the aisle.

For one thing, there was no aisle to march down. The members of the meeting would be seated in a circle in the plain room, and the bride and groom would walk in together and sit in the two chairs in front facing the others. Richard helped Ann down from their carriage. Their families entered and took their seats. Then, hand in hand, the couple walked in and seated themselves.

The meeting began in silence as was the custom. Ann forced herself to slow her breathing. Richard continued to gently hold her hand. Everyone was worshiping their God silently. After what seemed an eternity, Richard and Ann stood and faced one another. Taking both of Ann's hands in his, Richard proceeded to say in his deep voice, "In the presence of God and before these our families and friends, I take thee, Ann, to be my wife, promising with Divine assistance to be unto thee a loving and faithful husband so long as we both shall live.

Ann took a deep breath and looking into Richard's dark blue eyes, said, "In the presence of God and before these our families and friends, I take thee Richard to be my husband, promising with Divine assistance to be unto thee a loving and faithful wife so long as we both shall live. One of the three committee members stepped forward with the marriage certificate, and both Richard and Ann signed it.

The couple then took their seats once more, and the meeting continued in silence. After some time, a member stood and gave a word to the couple, another, followed, then another. Both sets of parents gave a short word of blessing.

Finally, a very old man stood and intoned, "Our God will bless thee and guide thy path forward. Walk in His ways and thou will walk in the light."

Silence followed for what to Ann seemed an eternity, then she noticed a committee member giving a signal with his hand, and the members stirred and started to rise. Chairs were cleared away, tables pulled out and a simple repast was served to those attending.

Finally, it was time for the bridal couple to depart. Richard helped Ann into the carriage, and they set out for the Sexton homestead. Ann could not remember the surrounding countryside ever to have been this beautiful before. The green grass and leaves were greener, the apple blossoms whiter, and the sky bluer than she had ever imagined. She was filled with joy. Richard pulled the carriage up to the front of the white house. Tethering the horse, he said to Ann, "I will take care of Ned here later. There is something more important to be done first."

Gathering her slight form up in his arms, he pushed open the front door and carried her over the threshold. Setting her gently down in this her new abode, he whispered, "Welcome home."

Ann sighed, *Here is the beginning of the rest of my life.*

Ann

1835 - 1848

MOTHERHOOD DELAYED

ANN PLACED A bowl of asters in the center of the table and stood back to admire her work. Finally, she was having her family to dinner. Five months had slipped by since her wedding day. Her early happiness had been marred by the death of Papa from pneumonia, just two months after the wedding. It had been a hard time for the family, but she threw herself into making this house the home she wanted. Everything had to be perfect before entertaining her family.

Right after the wedding, her bride's chest had been delivered and she happily unpacked all of the lovely items she had sewn over the years. She had smiled at her early efforts, but felt proud of all she had accomplished: sheets, pillowcases, towels, bureau scarves and doilies, even dish-towels came out of the chest and found their rightful place in her new home. Soon, she was busily engaged in sewing new curtains for all of the windows. Down came the heavy, dark drapes, up went the new airy coverings that let in the sunlight. She spent hours scrubbing, polishing, sorting and rearranging. When she felt she had done all she could, Ann set to planning the entertainment she had postponed.

Today, Mama, brother, Joseph and all of her seven sisters were coming for dinner. Next week it would be Richard's family's turn. The table was perfect, the wedding present china and her bride's chest table-cloth and napkins shining white underneath. Two plump hens roasted in the wood-stove oven together with potatoes rubbed with butter and winter squash topped with cinnamon. Greens simmered on the stove-top and fancy dishes of pickles and relish put up during the summer sat on the serving shelf. Ann had baked two apple pies for dessert. She felt proud of her accomplishments.

Richard came in from the field, gave her a kiss and eyeing the food, exclaimed. "What a feast, dear one. I can hardly wait!" He climbed the stairs to clean up from his chores.

Soon she heard the snorting of the horses and the clink of the har-ness as her family arrived. She opened the door wide to welcome them. She had seen her family often during the months since her wedding, but not all at the same time. Her mother and sisters came over to help with the canning and to sit with a cup of tea and gossip. Her brother she saw less often. This gathering gave her joy to have them all together once again. She only wished Papa could be there. Not long after the greeting and hugs, they all gathered at the table and Ann proudly carried in the juicy, golden hens, the glistening potatoes, squash and greens. The pickles, relishes, butter and jam already on the table, Ann ran back to the kitchen to fetch the yeasty rolls from the warming oven.

When all were seated, they all bowed their heads and offered a silent blessing on the food. Mama helped pass the dishes around. As each eagerly tasted the offerings, happy smiles spread on their faces. "This is wonderful, daughter!" Mama exclaimed.

"Yes, it is," echoed several of her sisters.

Joseph said simply, "Mmmm, Mmmm!"

That was good enough for Ann. She sat back and started to eat, happy as she thought possible. All that changed with her brother, Joseph's, question. "Is this a special occasion? Are we here to listen to a special announcement?"

Some of her sisters giggled at this. Ann felt a sinking in her stomach, and her appetite fled. Joseph with his teasing question was asking if there was a baby on the way already. Tears leapt to Ann's eyes. She wiped them away hastily.

Her mother looked at her in sympathy. "Joseph, it's very early yet to expect such an announcement. Ann and Richard have only begun to get used to being married."

One of the most important things Ann had looked forward to in being married was to have children. She knew several of her friends had babies just a short nine months after the wedding. However, the truth was that she had been so busy setting up her own precious and unique household that she had not thought much about it until her brother brought it up tonight. Her mother had talked to her before her wedding about the physical part of marriage. It did clarify her somewhat patchy knowledge of what *that* consisted of. Her mother's advice was something she knew she would have to endure if she wanted children, and at the time, it did not sit well with Ann. However, what actually transpired was indeed a surprise. Richard was patient, loving and gentle, and Ann found loving physically a very pleasurable thing, and not a task at all. She loved his closeness in their big four-poster bed. The little hugs and kisses snatched during their workday filled her heart with thankfulness. The children would come, she felt sure of that and in God's good time.

As Ann looked out her sitting room window, she noticed the leaves beginning to turn on the Sycamore trees. Another fall, the second since her marriage, almost a year to the day from the eventful dinner with her family. That had been a turning point for Ann. Ever since her brother's question about a possible pregnancy, Ann had considered the possibility. Every month, she would count the days to the time of her monthly blood and hope and pray that it would not come that time. But it did, regular as clockwork. As her friends had babies, one by one, some having already too close together, Ann felt her barren state more acutely. One day when her mother had stopped by, she had cried on her shoulder, bitter tears wrenched from her. Mama had patted her shoulder and told her to be patient, but on the next visit, she handed Ann a packet of herbs from the local midwife. "These are supposed to make thee conceive," Mama murmured. "It won't hurt to try them."

Ann mixed them in a tea and drank it religiously, but nothing happened. *Maybe we are not making love often enough,* she thought to herself. Richard was often so tired from the hard farm work that he fell asleep instantly when he crawled into bed. Ann would lie beside him listening to his gentle snores and wonder if she was missing the perfect time for conception.

Richard was not as happy and playful as he had been in the early days of their marriage. It had become apparent to Ann that he disliked farming. He seemed to love developing new seedlings and watching the fruit trees blossom and bear, but the long hours in the hay fields, planting, harvesting, storing, and the continuous demands of the livestock seemed to frustrate Richard immeasurably. Time spared from the demands of the farm often found Richard headed for town instead of spending time with a very lonely Ann. Thankfully, he did not head to the taverns but had a round he made to visit and argue with the local businessmen. He seemed to love the intellectual challenge of discussing new and innovative ideas. Ann felt left out and the greatest desire of her life, having children, seemed to be denied her. She sighed and put aside her needlework, this time a crochet project: medallions fashioned into a beautiful bedspread for their bed. Life would go on; the seasons would change one into another as God had planned and Ann felt she was facing a childless future.

Over three years passed with little change except that several times Ann missed her monthly time. It would be almost like holding her breath when it didn't happen. The small stack of clean flannel squares would sit in the drawer awaiting the onset, but one, two, three days passed without its appearance. After a week or ten days, Ann would let out her imagined held breath and begin to hope that she was indeed with child. She would say nothing to Richard until the second month had passed and twinges of nausea clenched at her stomach in the morning. Then sometime before the third missed month, the bleeding would start, and Ann knew it was over. Four times this happened to her, four times she had been bitterly disappointed. Ann remembered the last time this happened. After the blood and cramping had eased and she felt strong enough, she climbed a nearby hill one evening. It was a small and gentle hill, but she could see a long way from the top. She sat there a long time just feeling empty and alone. The sun began to slip beyond the horizon. A sunset began to form. She watched the sky changed from a faint pink to vibrant shades of magenta and orange. It took her breath away. The beauty of it stunned her, and she realized that no matter what her sorrow, the world was a beautiful place and she was thankful for it.

A few months later, she again missed her monthly time and set her mind up for another disappointment, but when she passed the third month without the usual spotting of blood, she began to hope that this would be different. Richard, too, began to hope that perhaps they might, at last after five years, have a child. As the little one grew within her, Ann relished every change in her body, and when she felt something like the flutter of a butterfly, she caught her breath in the wonder of it. As the months passed, she delighted in the baby's violent kicking and sometimes could even feel it having a fit of hiccups. The midwife had helped her calculate the date the baby should arrive on, but that day came and passed without anything happening. Ann thought, Baby dear, I have waited so long for thee, please come soon! Ann's mother spent days with her until Richard came in from work.

One morning as Ann boiled water to make tea she felt a sudden gush of water between her legs. "Mama, come quick, something is happening!"

Mama called to Richard, close by in the orchard. He ran to the house in great excitement. "It may be a while yet, but the baby is coming. Stay close to go for the midwife."

Mama got Ann cleaned up and into her nightgown. She watched her closely, and before long Ann's pains began. By noon, they were coming closer together, and Mama sent Richard for the midwife. She arrived an hour later. Ann felt that the pain would have her in its grip forever. Mama bathed her head in cool water and rubbed her arms soothingly, but when the pain took hold, she would think, *Did I really ask for this?*

Then the pains changed, and the midwife encouraged her to push with each one. One powerful pain engulfed her, and she pushed with all her might. Suddenly she felt she was being split in two.

"Just one more big push," the midwife coached. Ann complied and heard the beautiful words, "You have a baby boy!"

Soon his shrieks of protest rent the room. Ann thought she had never heard such a beautiful sound. She looked up at Mama and said, "I am going to name him William for my oldest brother."

"He will certainly be pleased to have a namesake," Mama replied.

William's arrival changed Ann's life as only a first baby can. He was healthy and to her, absolutely beautiful. She loved nursing him, bathing him, changing his diapers. The pretty layette her loving fingers had fashioned as she waited for his arrival looked so perfect on his small body. She spent hours just watching him sleep, his cradle close by her wedding bed. As he grew and changed and she witnessed the "firsts," she felt she was beholding a miracle and for her indeed it was.

When he first held up his head, smiled, laughed aloud, rolled over, sat up one by one Ann beheld these events and duly recorded them in a small book she kept at hand. She had her family over to celebrate

William's first birthday, and unbelievably that day, he took his first steps. Ann was delighted. A few months later when she realized another baby was on the way, she felt her "cup runneth over."

Baby Joseph arrived almost two years after his older brother. Richard insisted he be named for his father and several other Sexton ancestors. "You had your turn, now it's mine!" he laughed.

Richard was delighted with his beautiful, healthy sons after the childless years, but his dislike of farming had only grown in its intensity. He seemed to drag himself to do the everlasting chores, and Ann thought his apparent exhaustion had more to do with how he felt about the work than the actual work itself. Richard had met a man named Warren Henry Scudder, known as W. H. Scudder was a businessman and was impressed with Richard's business acumen which had been garnered by all of those conversations and arguments in town. W. H. came up with an idea and brought it to Richard one day. Richard was excited. He saw in W. H.'s proposal a way to get loose from the farming he hated.

One evening, he brought the proposal to Ann. "My friend wants me to go together with him and buy a general store in Dent." Dent was a village on the Harrison Pike.

"But it's too far from here," Ann said. "How would thee get back and forth."

"We would have to move," Richard replied. "There's a house near the store that is for sale. It isn't as big as this one, but we could make do."

Ann was taken aback by this fantastic proposal. "But, what about this house and farm?" Her voice rose.

"Our neighbor, Jed Barnes has spoken to me about leasing it, maybe buying it later."

Ann's voice shook with anger, "It seems that thee have planned all of this out just what thee want to do. What about me?"

Richard took a deep breath. "Ann, dear, I know you will like it and don't you want me to be happy, doing something I really want to do?"

Ann slept little that night. The children had sensed something was not right with their mother. William was hard to settle to sleep, and she was up with Joseph, nursing him more than was usual. Her whole life's dream was a home like this one with Richard, and now that the children were here, she felt she had everything she wanted. This radical change Richard proposed would upset everything. By morning, she had accepted the situation. Richard truly disliked farming. She loved Richard and wanted him to be happy.

As she faced her husband across the table at breakfast, she asked, "When do I get to see the house?"

Six years flew by. Ann could not believe it was now the year 1848. Two more children had been born into their family: George, named after her other brother, and at last a little girl, Elizabeth. As if in contrast to the four babies that were never to be born, these four were healthy and thrived on the early breast milk and later good food Ann gave them. The move to Dent had been hard, the house much smaller and soon filled to capacity with never still little ones. Ann remembered her lovely first home, how for so many years she strolled from room to room arranging cushions here, some flowers there. She realized how love had cut down the rooms one by one, but she felt that even so, she dwelt in a better house.

Ann's sister, Hannah, married Ephraim Fithian and Mama had moved in with them. Richard thrived in his business. He and W. H. made a good partnership. W. H. had a strong, solid business sense, Richard sparked entrepreneurial ideas by the dozens. People traveled miles to buy from them, knowing they would find a fair price and quality merchandise. Ann was pleased to see Richard so happy, but something of national importance would soon occur that would change many lives including the Sextons.

Word of the discovery of gold at a mill in far-off California soon reached the rest of the nation, even Ohio. The Cincinnati newspaper was full of the stories. Ann, busy with housework and caring for her little brood paid scant attention, but Richard and W. H. devoured every word.

Soon both were caught up in the frenzy of the times, becoming ever more excited about the possibilities. Some men they knew left for California, hoping to strike it rich and bring home a fortune. These treasure seekers left their wives and children behind to fend for themselves. Richard thought his proposal through carefully before approaching Ann.

One evening after returning home from the store and eating a simple supper with his family, Richard told the children to go to their rooms and play. He wanted to talk to their mother.

"What is it, husband?" Ann queried.

Richard plunged into the subject. "You have heard of the discovery of gold in California, how many are making their fortunes out there? I want to go. It is a wonderful opportunity."

Ann interrupted, "What in the world?"

"Just listen, please. I will not go alone as everyone else is. I could not stand to be apart from you and the children. I want us all to go together. Will you do this Ann?"

Ann was speechless. How could he even think of something like this?

"You don't have to give me an answer now. Just think about it. We will talk more tomorrow," Richard reassured her with a pat on her shoulder.

Ann sat stunned. She said nothing as she cleared up the supper dishes and washed them, then saw to the children getting ready for bed. When she finally climbed into bed next to the sleeping Richard, she lay there sleepless as thoughts raced through her head.

How can he ask this of me? I was twelve when I moved to western Ohio from New Jersey. That was to the far frontier, and now he wants to go to California, way, way out there on the other ocean? I would have to leave my family, my sisters, brother, mother, all of my friends, and what of the hardships of just getting there? Endless sea voyages or wagons rolling forever through mountains and deserts and what about Indian? They kill the travelers, even women and children. I just cannot do this!

Another morning across another breakfast table, Ann faced Richard over the oatmeal and coffee.

"I have my answer," she said in a quavering voice. "It's NO, absolutely not!"

Ann

1852

THE CALIFORNIA DECISION

THINGS DID NOT change noticeably in the Sexton household after Ann's ultimatum. Richard held his tongue for the most part, but if Ann sensed he might be leading up to the dreaded topic of California, she simply left the room. After all, there was plenty to do in her busy child-filled household. It seemed she was always washing, ironing, or mending.

Washday took all day with two large tubs in the backyard, heated over a fire and cooled to a bearable temperature with infusions of cold water. Ann bent over the washboard and earnestly applied the bar of homemade soap to a stair step of small trousers. Store keeping was easy on clothes, so Richard's clothes did not need much scrubbing now that he was no longer doing farming. Neither did little Elizabeth's dresses and pinafores, but oh, her boys! She made them change when they arrived home from school and she allowed their overalls to acquire a patina of dirt, before she gave up and doused them for a good scrubbing. The dirty clothes never seemed to end.

Ironing, too, took a whole day as she heated the smoothing irons on the stove and bent over the ironing board to press Richard's work shirts, the boys' smaller shirts and the little one's frilly clothing. She kept a careful and beautiful home, so she ironed tablecloths, napkins, towels and even sheets. She was proud of the fact that the family's underwear was beautifully ironed. No one could see them, but she knew how they looked beneath the clothing.

Mending was saved for the evening, when after supper the family gathered in the parlor, with Richard reading the paper and the children reading or playing games. Ann's senses were always on the alert during this time. She knew that every night Richard read the latest stories about the gold strikes in California. She glanced up from her sewing to the excited, alert look on his face and knew what was going on in his mind. Would he say something? Usually he did not, just sighed to himself, but if he looked her way and started to speak, she would put aside her current project and go into the kitchen where she always found something to do.

She could still not imagine going with all her children to that distant and frightening land. It was just asking too much. Surely Richard understood where she was coming from. She had a hard time understanding his excitement over this. The store was prospering. The farm sold finally to the neighbor who had leased it when they moved. Their financial situation was sound, but deep down she knew Richard's true makeup. He was restless, adventurous, always looking for a new challenge. Would he finally give up this ridiculous dream? She only hoped so.

Everything came to a head one day about a year and half after the first news of gold. Ann knew when Richard came home from the store that evening that something had happened. Richard's mouth was pulled into a thin line and a deep frown creased his brow. "What's wrong?" Ann asked, worry in her voice.

"Come, sit down, I need to talk to you," Richard replied.

Oh, no! Is someone in the family ill or worse yet, dead? Ann thought to herself.

"Dear Wife," he sighed. "I am losing my business partner. W. H. is going to California."

Ann sat back with dread surfacing as to what was coming next.

"He wants me to go with him. We would sell the store, of course. I told him I would not go without you and the children and so far you have refused to consider this idea. Please, dear one, tell me you might have changed your mind and would contemplate accompanying me as I have not given up on this dream."

Ann sat back, devastated. She thought through her words carefully, then spoke, "I know how much thou want to do this and I wish I could say yes without hesitation, but I simply cannot. I cannot responsibly commit my children to the risks that are involved and I cannot at this point bring myself to give up my life here with my family nearby. I hope thou can understand this."

Richard bowed his head and after a time nodded slowly. "I understand," he answered in what was almost a whisper. Ann felt tears surface. She did love him so much and did not want to disappoint him, but she found the proposal just impossible.

William, Joseph, and George were doing well in school, although they impatiently waited for classes to let out in order to indulge in all kinds of outdoor adventures. Ann acknowledged that the three were "all boy." Elizabeth was her little princess.

Elizabeth was just was about to enter school, when something quite unexpected happened in Ann's life. The children were spaced about two years apart and Ann considered her little family perfect. After Elizabeth, no new baby appeared on the scene and Ann was not particularly disappointed. She assumed that her childbearing, for whatever reason, was over. But as realization dawned on her that she was indeed again with child, she chided herself for ever assuming anything.

As soon as she was sure, she told Richard and could see the mixture of emotions race across his face. At first, delighted at the possibility of another little one, he soon realized that here was an even more potent reason for Ann to refuse to consider trekking to California.

The months of her pregnancy were surprisingly easy for Ann. There was no morning nausea as with the others and she seemed filled with boundless energy and good spirits. *Here*, she thought, *is my insurance for staying in Ohio. Oh, bless thou little one!*

However, as had happened to her before, the baby did not arrive at the calculated time. Ann decided not to sit around and notice every little bodily twinge and discomfort. She began cleaning house. It was a thorough cleaning, rugs were beaten, after the boys hauled them outside and onto the clothesline, windows were washed and floors scrubbed. She was sure she painted a strange picture with her protruding stomach, as she went about her work. She didn't bustle, the extra weight slowed her down, but she was determined and persistent. She sank into bed each night exhausted, but no labor pains started from all of her efforts.

Finally, the house was shining. "Time for thou to make thy entrance into the world, little one!" she exclaimed.

That night she awakened sometime after midnight with a strong contraction in her womb. It was a familiar feeling. She lay there, counting the time between the pains, Richard sleeping soundly beside her. Finally, she gently shook him by the shoulder and told him to go for the midwife. He was instantly wide awake and showed evidence of his intense excitement as he hurriedly dressed and got ready to leave. "Are you sure you will be all right until I can come back with the midwife? I can get Mrs. Grant from next door to come in.

"No, no," she gasped as another pain hit. "I know how I birth my babies. It will be a little while yet."

When Richard returned about three quarters of an hour later, the midwife got right to work.

It wasn't half an hour after that when a tiny life slid into the world and the midwife said once again, "You have a little boy." As they had discussed beforehand, he was named Lewis, because they both liked the name. As with her other children, he was beautiful and healthy and Ann was content.

One sunny afternoon, as Ann nursed little Lewis, she heard a carriage outside. Answering the knock on the door, she was surprised to see her sister, Hannah, there. Ann and Hannah had always been especially close, so she was delighted to see her and looked forward to spending time with her. Laying Lewis in his cradle, she took Hannah's bonnet and wrap and moved to the kitchen to put the kettle on for tea. Ann slid some slices of fruit bread onto a plate, poured the tea and carried a tray into the sitting room. "And what brings thou here today, dear sister?" she asked.

"Oh Ann, it's Ephraim," she sighed.

Oh no, Ann thought to herself. *They are having marital problems.* As it turned out, it was more complicated than that.

"Ephraim wants to go to California. In fact, he is determined to go and like thy Richard, he wants to take me and our child with him. I don't know what to do. I love him. I want to do what will make him happy, but I'm like you, I am really scared and I don't want to leave Mama. I know she is too old to make the trip."

Ann didn't know what to say. She had discussed her dilemma many times with Hannah and now here was Hannah facing the same problem. The sisters cried together, but that resolved nothing. Finally, Hannah left and Ann sat down with another cup of tea and examined her emotions. Her thoughts flew in all directions. She would now have an ally in her refusal, but what if, what if . . . she almost could not bring herself to think of the possibility, but what if they all went to California together? She would have another woman, her own dear sister, for company and help with the children.

When Richard came home and looked at the two tea cups, he knew that she had had company. "Who was here?" he asked."

"Hannah," Ann replied.

She did not elaborate, but from looking at Richard's face, she knew. He'd already talked to Ephraim. A suspicion arose in her mind. She wondered if Richard had talked Ephraim into going to California, hoping to get Hannah to agree and then talk Ann into it. Anger flared in Ann's chest. She hardened her heart saying to herself, *We'll see about that!*

Hannah came calling several times in the next few weeks and the discussion flew back and forth. All possibilities were explored. Ann could see Hannah was wavering. *She is going to go,* she realized at one point. The familiar sleepless nights returned. How many of these had she endured during her marriage as she contemplated another of Richard's adventurous schemes. Finally, she knew she had to make a decision. This was tearing her up and she could see Richard's worried face watching her. He knew of her dilemma.

She prayed, she thought, and argued with herself. Finally, she knew it was over. Then she could hardly wait for Richard to come home. When he pushed the door open, she took his hand and led him to a kitchen chair. As he sat down, she pulled a chair to face him and took both of his hands. "Richard, dear, I am ready to go to California with thou. Thou have never wavered in wanting this. I have never wavered in my love of thou and because I love thou, I want thou to have thy wish. I will go and the children too. It will be difficult. I have no illusions, but I will face the unknown and will endure what comes for thy sake. I love thou."

Richard sat speechless. Finally, he reached for her and pulled her into his arms. "Thank you, thank you. I will always try to honor your sacrifice."

Once it was settled, Ann actually began to feel excited about the coming adventure. Richard sold the store, realizing a fair profit. The house in Dent was for sale. They would not have a lack of finances for their trip, which was comforting. The packing was a challenge. Ann had five children to clothe as well as Richard and herself, but they could not take everything they wanted. Space on the ships would be limited and the trek across Central America would be a challenge. They had to travel light. Ann's beautiful linens from her bride's chest and her English china would have to be left behind. She parceled these between her sisters. Instead, plain metal plates, cups and forks were packed, as were a couple of cooking pots.

Richard brought tinned and dried food from the stock at the store to take. "They are supposed to furnish meals, but I think we would be wise to bring our own as much as possible. The conditions might mean food would be contaminated."

Finally, one day in July, the packing was complete, the family visited, the goodbyes all said. Ann's brothers drove the two families, the Fithians and the Sextons to the stage coach station. Two couples and six children were ready to leave everyone and everything they had known and set out for a strange land as many had before. Ann clutched her bag and pulled six-month-old Lewis closer to her. She shivered slightly. Here it was, her first step into the unknown. Was she ready for this? She truly did not know.

The Journeys

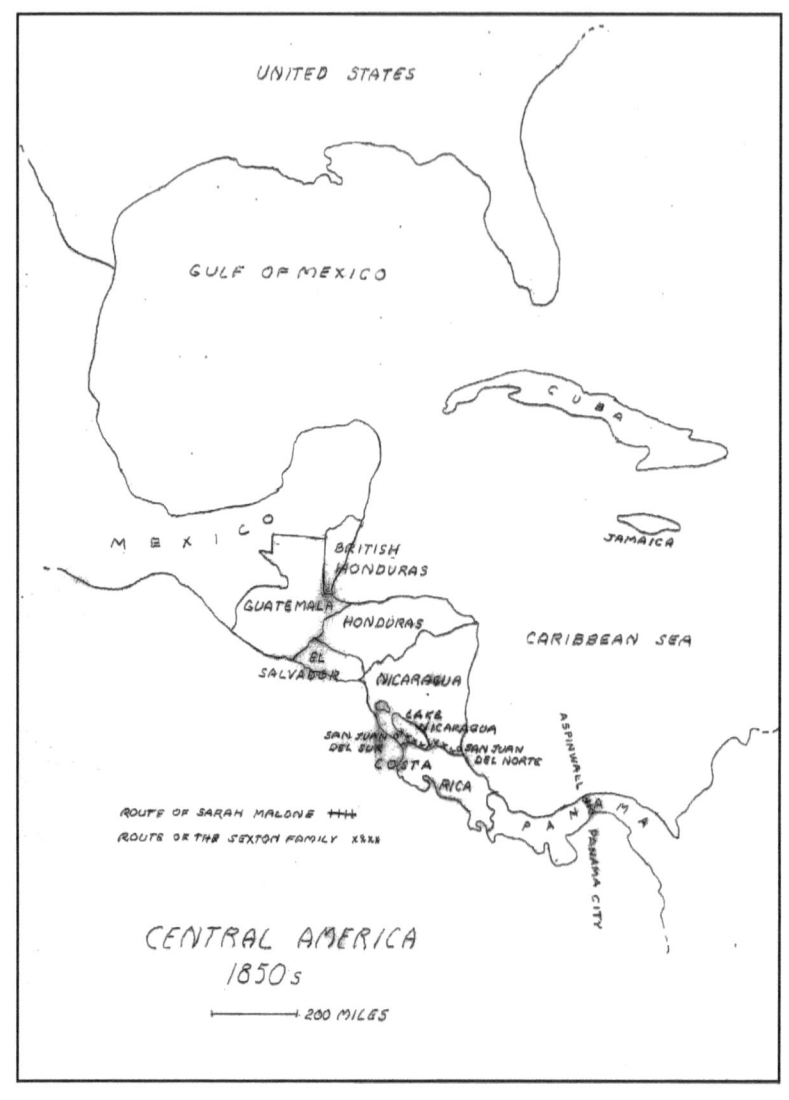

UNITED STATES

GULF OF MEXICO

CUBA

JAMAICA

MEXICO

BRITISH HONDURAS

GUATEMALA

HONDURAS

CARIBBEAN SEA

EL SALVADOR

NICARAGUA

LAKE NICARAGUA

SAN JUAN DEL SUR

SAN JUAN DEL NORTE

COSTA RICA

ASPINWALL

PANAMA

PANAMA CITY

ROUTE OF SARAH MALONE ┼┼┼
ROUTE OF THE SEXTON FAMILY x%%x

CENTRAL AMERICA
1850s

├───────┤ 200 MILES

CENTRAL AMERICA, 1850

$\mathcal{A}nn$

Delays

THE THREE DAYS by stagecoach to Cleveland were surprisingly uneventful. When Richard had first proposed taking this route, Ann expressed doubts as it seemed so out of the way, but Richard researched the travel options carefully. As he explained it to her, she saw the wisdom of it. Instead of seventeen or eighteen long days by stagecoach to New York, they would travel to the shores of Lake Erie, take the steamer the length of the lake, then another seven days by stage on the northern route from Buffalo to New York City, a total of eleven days. Ann relied on Richard's intelligent thinking in the planning of this trip.

Arriving at the dock on Lake Erie, Ann took a good look at the steamer that would cross the lake. It was the first ship of this size she had size. It was impressive. Little did she know that their luck was about to change for the worse.

As the families boarded along with their luggage, and the engines started in preparation for departure, suddenly, the ship began pitching in a violent motion. A hawser had caught in one of the paddle-wheels. The crew tried in vain to extricate it but were unsuccessful. Ann clasped baby Lewis to her and grabbed for Elizabeth. Her stomach lurched, but looking at her children's slightly green faces, she forgot about her discomfort. The boys leaned over the rail and promptly threw up their breakfasts. Poor Elizabeth was too short to reach the rail and vomited on her dress. Ann tried to clean her up as best she could, but then became violently sick herself. *This is awful!* she thought.

They were finally on their way, but still had to sail against a stiff gale the entire day, all the way to Buffalo. The feeling of nausea never left the family members, but thankfully, soon there was nothing left on their stomachs to lose. As they disembarked, some were still choking back the gagging reflex. It took a while to feel that the ground had stopped moving.

They found an inn to stay the night which gave them a chance to recuperate and the next morning they boarded another stagecoach which would take them to New York City. As anticipated, this took about a week, stopping each night at an inn along the way. Soon these stops began to blend into each other in Ann's mind as there was little to differentiate them. The accommodations were adequate, and the food was plain but filling. But Ann felt a sense of excitement as they arrived in New York City. It was the biggest city she had ever seen.

The bustle of the waterfront was breathtaking. So many ships docked in every available space. There were sailing ships and newer steamships even anchored out in the bay. Ann wondered which one would be taking them to Panama.

Delmonico's had built some hotels near the waterfront in order to accommodate the massive influx of travelers to California. The two families were able to find space in one of them, and they settled in for the night after a filling meal in the dining room.

"I'll go to the steamship office in the morning to book our passage," Richard announced.

"I will accompany you," Ephraim interjected.

"Good! We need to get going as soon as possible."

The next morning, Ann felt revived and hopeful. They all had bathed the night before and a good night's sleep. She washed out Lewis's diapers and some of the children's clothes, hoping they would be dry in time to repack if Richard and Ephraim returned with the tickets.

Around noon, she heard the key turn in the hotel room door, and Richard came in. "Did thou get the tickets?" she queried. "When do we leave?"

"There is a problem," Richard sighed. "There are so many passengers wanting to go to California, many more than there is room for. They are putting more people on each ship than it should hold. However, the real problem comes in is that we all want to travel together, and there are ten of us, counting baby Lewis."

Disappointment showed on Richard's face, and Ann put her arms around him. "Well, we will just wait until there is room," she assured him.

Ann resigned herself to waiting, but she could not help hoping each day as Richard returned from the docks that he would have good news and they could leave. The children ran out of things to do in their hotel room, and the areas near the docks were crowded and dangerous. She could not let the boys roam the streets. Devising new games to play, pictures to be drawn, or books to be read had about run their course. After a little over a week, Richard suggested that they find a boarding house to stay in which would be less expensive and in a better area. He took a hansom cab to explore the possibilities and came back with good news that he had found one with rooms for all of them as the previous boarders had just left for California. Ann repacked and they all loaded into several cabs for the ride further up the island to Mrs. Bland's Boarding House.

Their landlady was friendly, she was a good cook, and they all felt comfortable there. However, Ann hoped that their stay would not be long—she was anxious to get on with their journey.

It was not to be, however. July was over and August crept by with its intense heat and humidity. Early September was not much better, but toward the end of the month it cooled off. Ann started taking the children on excursions to the center of Manhattan where there was still a wild, wooded area. They would take the horse trolley and the tickets were only five cents each. Mrs. Bland packed them a picnic lunch in a basket, and they enjoyed eating on the grass under the trees. The older children ran and explored; Lewis kicked on the blanket. William, twelve, Joseph, ten, and George, eight, were ecstatic with so much to explore and trees to climb. Elizabeth, almost six, built little rooms for her doll out of leaves and branches. These short trips made the days bearable. Sometimes, Hannah, with little Matilda, also came along, and Ann delighted in the conversation and company. [These woods that meant so much to Ann would later become Central Park.]

As the days grew shorter and cooler, the leaves on the trees started to turn. Ann always loved this time of year and sometimes homesickness would overcome her as she thought of Ohio, which she knew she had left forever. By October there was a definite chill in the air. She laid out wraps for the children and herself before venturing out. She put her expectations on hold as the days marched on and when Richard returned from the docks each afternoon, she could tell by his face that the news was discouraging.

It came as a complete surprise when he finally burst excitedly into the boarding house parlor and shouted, "We're going. We're going! At last, we're going. All of us!"

Ann jumped up, the children gathered around her.

"We will be leaving in two days, on October twentieth on a Vanderbilt ship called the *Star of the West*. It is her inaugural voyage to Nicaragua. I have paid for first-class passage to San Juan del Norte in Nicaragua. We will reach there in eight days time. Our passage is paid for—all the way to San Francisco!"

Ann felt she was dreaming. After a three month wait, they were sailing in two days. "Why Nicaragua?" Ann queried.

Richard replied, "Commodore Vanderbilt has started this new line,

The Accessory Transit Company. The Star of the West is a new ship, and best of all, the fare is only $150 a person, almost half the cost of the other line."

Ann found all of this hard to take in. Her mind flew to the tasks she needed to accomplish in the short time remaining, and she felt a thrill of excitement course through her. "We are actually going!" she exulted.

Early on the morning of October 20, 1852, the Sexton and Fithian families boarded the gleaming new side wheeler, *Star of the West*. It was docked at the foot of Bowling Green, just off Broadway, north of the Battery. While the ship was loaded to capacity and beyond, the families boarded and found their cabins to be spacious and comfortable. Elizabeth and baby Lewis shared a bunk; George and Joseph another. William had his own as he had started sprouting up at an amazing rate and took up one all by himself. As for Ann, she tucked her small body next to Richard's in one bunk. There were curtains in front of the bunks, a washstand occupied one corner, and there was a space for storage of luggage. All in all the accommodations were quite adequate. The toilets were shared and located at the end of the row of deck cabins.

The dining hall formed an open area between the rows of first-class cabins. It held a long table and benches. Meals were served there three times a day and also provided a space for relaxing and visiting. The top deck offered open air and views of the shore as the ship proceeded south. The crisp October chill began to disappear, and warmer weather appeared as the journey progressed. Both in the dining area, and on the top deck, an air of sociability prevailed. Women visited with each other as they watched their children. Some read, some others played board games.

The food was above passable, so the Sextons decided to save their stash of tinned goods and jarred preserves packed in a carry case for future needs. This would prove to be a wise decision. Breakfast might consist of omelets or hot cakes; sometimes buckwheat cakes served with butter and honey. Lunch would usually be freshly baked bread with cheese, pickles and perhaps sardines. Dinner supplied a variety of meats such as chicken, ham, or lamb with potatoes green peas, corn or green beans and cake or pudding for dessert. Always there was a liberal supply of coffee and tea.

The one negative and quite overwhelming problem was the noise from the adjacent first-class cabins. Ann was told that gambling on the ships in the past had taken over all of the decks to the detriment of ordinary family passengers. In order to contain this, it was now limited to individual cabins where men gathered and noisily pursued their luck into all hours of the night. Ann also noticed some brightly dressed women with flamboyant attitudes and loud, raucous voices entering these cabins. She assumed that these were not nice women and avoided them in the public areas. Men were undoubtedly in the vast majority, but there was perhaps a couple of dozen "loose women." Families with children were definitely in the minority.

During the day, most of the passengers passed the time on deck under a large canvas awning. The crisp days of autumn soon turned warmer as they sailed south. They traveled close to the coast from New York to Cape Hatteras. The ship skillfully navigated this dangerous area, then lost sight of the coastline. By the time they sailed between Cuba and Florida, the humidity became stifling. Heading south again between the tip of Cuba and Mexico, they knew they were nearing their destination.

[The Sextons had no way of seeing into the future, but the *Star of the West*, whose inaugural voyage they experienced, would play a fascinating role in U.S. history. On January 9, 1861, the ship was fired upon in Charleston Harbor by cadets from the Citadel. The ship was withdrawing from the harbor when it was hit twice by guns from Fort Moultrie. These were the first shots fired in the Civil War. On April 18, 1861, she was captured by the Confederates in Matagorda Bay and sailed to New Orleans. Two days later *The Star* became a hospital ship for the Confederacy. Still later, when union Forces took New Orleans, she escaped recapture and fled up the Mississippi River. Around April 10th, 1863, she was sunk broadside in the Tallahatchie River to block Union gunboats which were attacking Vicksburg.]

October 28th dawned hot and humid as the ship neared the Nicaraguan coast. Ann had all their belongings neatly packed, including Lewis's freshly washed diapers, bibs, and dresses. The passengers gathered on deck as they approached land. Ann had enjoyed this ocean voyage in spite of the noisy nights. She made some new friends, as did the children and everyone experienced a good time. Even Lewis seemed content. The wait in New York had been frustrating, but now they were well on their way. Ann felt optimistic about the rest of the trip, however her optimism was sorely misplaced.

The ship drew closer to shore. Ann looked out on an unbelievable sight. Hundreds of canoes came rowing out to meet them, manned by brown skinned natives. As if that were not an amazing sight in itself, there were dozens of other native men, stripped to their waists, wading out into the water. She observed all of this in wonderment, not quite believing what she was seeing.

Turning to Richard, she asked, "Where are the docks?"

Ann

October November 1852

Nicaragua

THE SCENE THAT confronted Ann was breathtaking. A large sandbar stretched across the harbor, blocking any large ship from docking at San Juan del Norte. Indeed, there were no docks, so in order for cargo and passengers to reach the shore, they either had to be loaded into small boats called bungos or carried on the muscled backs of natives. Their skin ranged in color from black to bronze, and they were only clothed from the waist down.

Ann looked on in horror. *I will not climb on the back of one of those naked men,* she vowed.

Her boys held no such reservations and with wild hilarity were borne to shore in this manner. Before wading out on his own, Richard waited with Ann until a bungo with enough room took his wife, Elizabeth, and Lewis toward the shore. They waited some time for their luggage to arrive by both means of transportation.

San Juan del Norte was called Greytown by the English, and it still appeared much more a pirate than a traveler's town. There were many cases of fever in town at that time, and Ann was relieved that they would not be staying there for long.

The heat and humidity were overpowering. Ann felt as if she were wrapped in a very wet wool blanket. She found it hard to breathe.

On shore, she noticed many small insects were attacking them, and she covered Lewis as best she could. Once they were all gathered together with their belongings, more natives carried their luggage to one of the nearby hotels. They managed to secure one room for all of them and found they had hammocks for beds with billows of mosquito netting surrounding each one. The rooms were quite open, and there were no toilets, just an open latrine down a path with only a short wall for privacy. The floor of their room was sand and the walls discolored with a variety of unidentifiable dirt. What with the heat, bugs, and noise, Ann barely slept that night. She was relieved to find out the next morning that they had a place on the boat up the San Juan River. It was leaving in an hour. She could not wait to be out of this dirty, diseased town.

It was the end of the rainy season, but there still was a heavy downpour several times a day. The San Juan River was flowing fairly well, and the Sexton's small boat found its way up the river and over the rapids with only minor difficulties. Ann viewed the jungle on the shore with interest. Never had she seen such dense vegetation. Strange plants grew tall and were the most vibrant green she had ever seen. Someone pointed out banana plants with huge leaves and bunches of green fruit. Some small animals moved through the trees. These turned out to be spider monkeys. The children were fascinated by their antics. The ear-shattering cry of howler monkeys tore through the vegetation, a sound she would not soon forget.

Ann noticed what appeared to be brown logs on the banks but suddenly saw that some were moving. "What are those?" she gasped?

"Those are crocodiles," one of the other passengers replied.

A shiver of fear ran up Ann's spine. One time they had to get off the boat and walk a few hundred yards. Ann held her breath as they made their way past the ugly beasts and slowly let out her breath as they completed the portage to a new boat. They arrived at the town of San Carlos in the afternoon and spent a night in what was almost an exact duplicate of the hotel of the previous night. In spite of the discomfort, Ann slept a sleep of pure exhaustion, but woke up drenched in sweat and attacked by a swarm of mosquitoes biting her on her face, neck, and hands. Ann made all of the children pull their sleeves down over their hands and cover the back of their necks, but still, they had bites on their faces. The children were uncomfortable and complained of the heat and the itching. Lewis was fussy and did not calm down as he usually did when she nursed him.

That morning they boarded a small shallow-draft steamer to cross Lake Nicaragua. It took them the seventy-five miles across to La Virgen on the western shore of the lake. Lake Nicaragua was a very shallow lake, and the captain navigated the ship skillfully to avoid running aground. The trip took all day. They saw more crocodiles on the shore and floating in the lake. As if they were not frightening enough, bull sharks flashed through the water. These were huge, up to six feet in length. Sometimes the passengers would spot saw-fish, and Ann wondered if other monsters were hiding in the water. There were several rain squalls which did not lower the temperature at all. If anything it was even hotter and more humid. Ann was grateful that the bug population seemed to decrease as they moved through the water. The food served on the ship was very poor, so Richard took some tinned fish and crackers out of their supply to carry them over. The children gulped these down hungrily.

They finally docked at La Virgen, another small, filthy town and found themselves with even worse accommodations as the rooms were exceedingly dirty. *Only one night here,* Ann thought, *I can do this for one night.* The next morning they expected to board a stagecoach for the short journey over the mountain to San Juan Del Sur, where they would meet their ship bound for San Francisco, California. *I can get through this, and then we will be on our ship.* She hoped the ship would be a newer one like the *Star of the West* and the long voyage up the coast equally as pleasant as that one.

After pulling their possessions together and getting themselves as ready as possible, they trooped to the stagecoach station. They soon found the stagecoach had been delayed. No one seemed to know when the next one would arrive. The adults held a brief conference. The fear was that this unforeseen delay would put them behind schedule and they had a ship to meet. They arrived at an alternative plan. They would hire mules and natives to guide them and take this mode of transportation over the mountain. This put them some behind but still would get them there in time to board the ship. Everyone agreed to this and set out to find mules and their owners as soon as possible.

As luck would have it, there were not enough mules to go around, so Richard hired a native to carry George on his back. Another lady wanting to get to San Juan del Sur hired another native to carry her daughter.

Instead of waiting for the rest of the party, the two natives took off on a jog. Ann screamed, "Stop! Stop!"

It was to no avail, the natives were on their way and did not listen. Quite possibly they did not understand English and just ignored this crazy white lady.

Ann started sobbing. "My little boy, I've lost him." Joseph, already seated on a mule, started to follow the pair. The little girl's mother soon joined him, and off they went.

Ann became even more distraught. "No, Joseph! I don't want to lose thou too!" Ann's heart was beating so hard, and her breath was coming so rapidly, she thought she might have a heart attack. "Richard, do something!"

The remaining party started on the muddy trail up the mountain. Ann rode her mule mindlessly with tears streaming down her face. She pictured a disaster happening to her two sons. *Going to California was the worst decision I have ever made! If I lose my two boys, I will never forgive Richard for talking me into this!.* The relatively short time on the trail seemed to take forever. Ann did not even notice the rain or the bugs, she just prayed, *Please, oh God, save my boys!*

Finally, they reached the crest of the mountain and could see the Pacific Ocean down below them. As the trail wound down to the town of San Juan del Sur, Ann found herself almost faint from fear. The party looked right and left as they entered the town. "There they are!" Richard shouted joyfully. Indeed, there were George and Joseph, as well as the woman and her small daughter. Only one mule stood nearby. It seemed Joseph had run his mule into a bog which sucked the animal down into its depths. Joseph had managed to walk out and continued over the mountain on foot.

Ann cringed at hearing this near-death story, but she was so relieved to find her sons and have her family together at last, that all she could do was whisper, "Thank you, thank, God!" through her tears.

Once the family had collected their members and belongings, they made their way to yet another hotel. This one the worst of the lot. It did not matter to Ann. A terrifying experience had ended well, and she could breathe again. Ann noticed that there was no ship in sight, but at the time, this did not trouble her either. Communications being what they were in 1852, the Sextons had no way of knowing that their ship still sat in San Francisco Bay under a cholera quarantine.

Ann

NOVEMBER 1852-JANUARY 1853

THE LEWIS

THE OPPRESSIVE DAYS dragged by in San Juan del Sur. The Sextons were not the only passengers waiting for a ship to arrive to take them to California. There were hundreds like them and each day brought more. Every day dawned already sticky with heat and humidity and Ann would think, *Maybe today, the ship will come and we can leave this horrible place.* But the day only gave back an unbroken view of blue water. Ann had managed to clean their small room to some extent, scrubbing the filthy walls with salt water. The communal latrine was hopeless, however, and the family members held their breath when using it.

Food had become a problem. There was fruit in abundance, and they enjoyed the bananas, mangoes, figs and other strange delicacies, but mainstays, such as meat and bread were practically nonexistent.

Sometimes, Richard managed to secure a locally caught fish which Ann cooked over the small stove they had assembled in their room. She was thankful for the cooking utensils they brought with them and more and more, they fell back on the tinned and bottled supplies they carried from Ohio.

Six weeks passed and Ann gave up looking out for a ship to arrive. One day she sensed something different going on in the town. She wasn't sure whether it was the sound of raised voices or a vibration in the air, but she ran out of their room and looked toward the Pacific. There it was! At last a ship stood out against the horizon. Richard was down at the shore watching the children as they played in the water. Ann picked up *Lewis* and ran to find them. "It's here, it's here," she called as she saw her family. All of them had already spotted the ship. The children were jumping up and down with excitement. Now there was hope of leaving this downtrodden village.

The ship was the *Samuel S. Lewis*, a mainstay of Vanderbilt's Independent Line, as he called his Pacific Coast route between California and Nicaragua. The ship had a rather radical design. It was propeller driven rather than a side wheeler. The through-hull fittings for the propeller shaft leaked and got much worse if the shaft got out of alignment.

When new, it had an auspicious beginning. On September 16, 1851 it participated in a grand jubilee on Boston Harbor to celebrate the completion of the first railroad linking Boston and Canada. President Millard Fillmore and other dignitaries including Daniel Webster toured the harbor aboard the *Lewis*. She then sailed for England and back, but encountered difficulties and never again attempted a transatlantic voyage. The *Lewis* was sold to Vanderbilt in 1852 and he readied her for the Pacific Coast run. Her first run saw nineteen deaths on the voyage and complaints were rampant. Vanderbilt sold the ship, but was forced to lease her back and now she sat in the harbor of San Juan del Sur waiting to take on passengers.

The passengers presented a huge problem. There were too many of them. All of these had bought tickets through to San Francisco on this ship, so it was either get aboard or lose their fare, forcing them to pay for passage on another ship. The crush to get on the *Lewis* was powerful. The Sextons and Fithians managed to board, but at a cost in comfort and privacy. They would have to share their cabins with other passengers on a rotation basis for use of the bunks. A schedule was set up for this. Ann could not bear to sleep between sheets shared with other unwashed passengers, so she told her family to just lie on top of the bedding. In the heat, this was not a problem.

What was much more difficult to deal with was the stench. "Whew, what a smell!" William gasped. Little Elizabeth started gagging.

Ann pulled handkerchiefs and squares of flannel from their luggage and tied them over the children's noses and mouths. This seemed to help. The smell came from rotting garbage and from the filthy toilets they were forced to use. It seemed no one had made an effort to clean this ship in preparation for the upcoming voyage.

"We will just have to do the best we can with this awful situation," Ann spoke to her children. "Do not touch anything when thou use the toilet and come back immediately to the cabin and wash thy hands." Ann had foreseen that fresh water might be in short supply and had brought salt water soap with her.

At last, overcrowded to the greatest possible extent, the ship was underway. There was very little distinction between first class, second class and steerage due to the overcrowding. Many were sleeping on the decks themselves, every possible inch of space occupied. No pleasant dining hall experience on this trip, meals were served from large pots onto plates or bowls. Some, like the Sextons had brought their own utensils. They were the lucky ones as others had to use what was passed on by those further up in line, without the benefit of a washing.

The six weeks in San Juan del Sur had depleted the Sextons supply of tinned food, except for a very few jars of homemade preserves and pickles, which Ann had hidden among their clothing, saving them for an emergency. They were forced to eat the ship's food. It was terrible. Except for the fresh fruit from San Juan del Sur which only lasted the first couple of days, the food was the same twice a day. This consisted of a concoction called lobscouse. It was made of a hash of potatoes, salt pork, and hard tack. It was greasy and it smelled. At first the children refused to eat it, but soon changed their minds as their hunger became unbearable. They even became excited over a dessert served very occasionally called dandy funk. This was hard tack broken up and boiled in molasses, sometimes with cinnamon and raisins added. The last two ingredients soon disappeared and soon there was no more dandy funk at all.

The ship put in at Acapulco in Mexico after five days at sea. This stop replenished the supplies with fresh water and fruit and passengers were picked up who had taken the land route across Mexico. Ann failed to see how any more people could be squeezed onto this vessel. It was apparent, soon after leaving San Juan del Sur, that some of the passengers were quite ill. Word spread through the passengers that someone had died the day before docking at Acapulco. It was said it was a man from Missouri named Threkeld. Ann watched his shrouded body being carried down the gangplank when they docked. He would be buried there. Ann felt sad for this man and wondered who would tell his family back in Missouri.

As they sailed away from Acapulco, Ann knew there were seventeen more days on this poisonous ship before they arrived in San Francisco. The passengers welcomed the fresh fruit and water, but that did not last long with so many people on board, a number swelled even more with the Mexico passengers. Ann coped as best she could. She washed Lewis's diapers in buckets of salt water with salt water soap. Even thorough rinses did not remove the salty irritant, and the baby's bottom became a raw, red rash. Ann pulled out her tin of lanolin and smeared a coating of this on his posterior. In a few days, the rash cleared up. The children were good about wearing their masks and washing their hands after toileting and before eating. Ann just hoped her supply of salt water soap would last the whole trip.

The food was getting even less palatable, and bugs began to appear in the *lobscouse*. The occasional beans they were served were even more infested. At first disgusted, the children soon began to make a game out of how many bugs they could pick out of the food. When things became unbearable, Ann pulled out a jar of pickles or sweet preserves and surreptitiously divided these up with her family. She knew that other passengers with similar rations had been selling these treats to others for as much as a dollar a pickle. Keeping her family's morale up was worth much more than this to Ann. The water became almost undrinkable, but even so was now rationed as the supply grew ever more scant. When squalls of rain occurred, barrels were placed on deck to catch the rainwater, but it was never enough. Water standing for a long time in wooden casks became stagnant and gave off a terrible odor. Pitchers of water would hold several inches of a filthy sediment in the bottom. Sometimes the water was made more palatable by adding a mixture of molasses and vinegar, but eventually, even these supplies ran out, and the water was consumed in spite of the smell.

General morale among the passengers sank to a new low. As conditions deteriorated, tempers flared, and a general feeling of rage took hold of the populace. With this came bouts of profanity which steadily escalated until it was impossible to escape the foul language. The more devout among the throng listened to this with a great feeling of dismay. They felt that the prevailing sounds of blasphemy would surely bring down the wrath of the Almighty upon this unfortunate vessel and they would sink into the depths with all on board perishing.

A meeting of the faithful was called. Many showed up including some not so faithful, but tired of the ongoing cursing. A petition was drawn up and signed calling for a cessation of profanity. Unfortunately, it had little effect as had a previous petition to have the cook fired and replaced. To Ann, it made little difference, she was committed to this test of endurance on what she considered to be her family's prison.

Illness was now rampant on the ship. Several had undoubtedly caught the "Panama" fever (Yellow fever) in San Juan del Sur, but the terrible conditions on the ship surely sickened others. Deaths seemed to become a regular occurrence.

Three days out of Acapulco, a Mr. Shea from Illinois died of fever and diarrhea. His body was unceremoniously slipped into the churning water of the Pacific. Two days later on December 24th, the fever claimed another victim, a Mr. Elliott of Toronto, Canada. The next day, another slid into the sea, two days later another. On December 20, two died, one, a J.C. Greene of Carlisle, Pennsylvania was only twenty-three years old. In all, eleven died on the trip to San Francisco. Mr. Greene was not the youngest. That was Jacob Trantree, age eighteen of Wayne County, Ohio. Mr.Trantree's death hit very close to home, not only because he was so young, but because his home was so near her own back in Ohio.

Each death brought sorrow to Ann's tender heart. All those dreams come to nothing. As the last person died the day they arrived off San Francisco, Ann realized that all of the dead were men. This amazed her. She felt so thankful that her family had been protected. There had been some small upsets, which had struck fear into her heart, but each quickly recovered. Each time she thanked God.

As the ship plowed shakily north, the weather cooled. At last, it was quite cold with frequent bitter fog. Ann put warm wraps on the children. One day seemed much like another, but one morning Ann realized that it was Christmas Day. It seemed foolish to acknowledge this as every day was just another test of fortitude and the sameness was stultifying. How she wished she had planned better and brought some small gifts for the children, but she had thought they would be in San Francisco well before Christmas. She vowed she would make it up to them when they were settled.

New Years Day a week later did not even merit a thought, but the hope of seeing land in two days' time overshadowed everything. The ship itself was in an incredibly leaky condition. Water built up and sloshed around below decks. As they neared San Francisco on January 2, 1853, the shaft finally broke. And they were out of coal. The ship lay twenty-five miles off San Francisco unable to move. All hope seemed to drain from the passengers. *This cannot be,* thought Ann. *So near, but so far. Will this nightmare ever end?* It was another two days before the ship *Goliah* towed the *Lewis* to the Embarcadero.

The *Lewis's* next voyage would be its last. Eighteen days out of San Juan del Sur with 385 passengers on board, it missed San Francisco Bay in a thick fog and shortly before daylight ran aground at Bolinas Bay, eight miles to the north. The passengers and cargo were landed safely, including a famous passenger, William Tecumseh Sherman. The Lewis, however, was a total loss. The *Alta California* noted succinctly that "…this loss may be considered as rather beneficial to the traveling public…" As for Vanderbilt, the poor conditions of his Pacific line caused him to be hung in effigy in San Francisco on a regular basis.

As Ann stepped onto the Embarcadero with her family, she could still feel the rocking of the ship and smell the awful stench. Her clothes smelled and were filthy as were those of the rest of the family. *I do not think that a multitude of washings will ever remove this smell!* And thus went Ann's welcome to her new home.

Sarah

A JOURNEY ALONE

SNOW BLANKETED THE countryside as the stagecoach left Fort Wayne, Indiana. The miles crept by. Sarah gazed out the window at the barren trees and grey skies. She shivered and wrapped her shawl more closely around her. She briefly gave thanks for the other three passengers as their body heat helped warm the coach interior. It was a lengthy trip—seventeen days to New York City. Sarah had not allowed herself to feel sad at saying goodbye to the Hirsch's. She merely willed herself to feel nothing at all, knowing if she thought about it too much, she would be overwhelmed. *Later, maybe,* she whispered as she laid her head against the wall of the coach. In minutes she was asleep.

In the early afternoon, they stopped at an inn. She ate a bowl of hot and tasty stew. Two of the Fort Wayne passengers left, another three boarded, and the horses pulled away from the inn on the icy roads. Nightfall found them at another inn. After a meal very similar to the one at noon, the passengers went to their rooms. Sarah shared a room with two other women. As she lay down on the hard pallet on the floor in her clothes, she marked the first day of her journey down in her mind.

Every day seemed a replica of the one before. Little changed in the scenery: snow-covered hills, bare trees, an occasional small town, fields, farmhouses, barns, and animals.

The inns were much the same, with little to distinguish one from another in either sleeping accommodations or food. Passengers got off; new ones got on. Most looked all alike to Sarah. She did not talk to her neighbors except to greet them politely or tell them goodbye. However, there was one exception. An older woman boarded in a nameless town along the way. She seemed confused and tried to ask the man next to her a question, who looked at her in a bewildered manner. The woman, realizing he did not understand her, looked crestfallen and frightened.

Sarah realized the woman was speaking Yiddish and that she did not speak English. Sarah spoke to her gently in Yiddish, "Megn ikh bahilfik du?"–*May I help you?*

When she realized that Sarah could answer all her questions the woman, tiny and wizened in her shabby shawl, was so relieved that she could be understood that she latched onto Sarah. They shared a room that night, and Sarah thought her companion would never stop talking. Grateful that she could be of help, Sarah nevertheless felt a sense of relief when the woman left the stagecoach in a town the next day. She was greeted by a large family, hugging and exclaiming in Yiddish and Sarah was overwhelmed with homesickness. She could not help the rain of tears that coursed down her cheeks.

Sarah became overwhelmed and dam broke, and she let her emotions sweep over her, thinking of the Hirsch's and the love they had shown her. How she wished she could have stayed in that warm nest! Her thoughts flew even further back to the cabin in the woods and her hopes and dreams of becoming a teacher that was shattered by Ma's death. She was only fifteen. The two years at the Hirsch's had been a wonderful gift. Sarah allowed herself to dream again, thinking of opening her own tailor shop in Fort Wayne. Now, here she was on this stagecoach flying forward into an unknown future.

She smiled as she heard Isaac Hirsch uttering one of his favorite sayings in her mind, "A mentsh tracht und Gott lacht."–*A person plans and God laughs.*

Dear Isaac! Maybe she should just not ever plan. It certainly seemed to do no good.

This introspection brought on other thoughts. Sarah missed her sister Katie. She could not bare the thought that she might never see her again. But [1]Katie had no wish to travel to California. She had found a niche for herself in Fort Wayne. Like Sarah, Katie thrived in the Nerdlinger home. She bested Sarah by learning both Yiddish and German. She was fluent in both. She also possessed a beautiful soprano voice. Once this became known, she was asked to sing at many public functions. A Protestant minister, hearing her sing at one of these performances, persuaded her to sing at his church. The congregation loved her voice, and soon she decided to join the church. Katie was the first of the Malone sisters to desert her Roman Catholic faith. Now she was attracting the attentions of a young ministerial student named Reasoner. Yes, Katie was firmly entrenched in the American Midwest. Sarah felt sad. She missed her already.

Sarah's thoughts flew out to California to her other two sisters, Maria and Maggie. Oh, how she hoped she would see Maria again, that she would survive this illness and recover. Little Maggie, now fourteen, was evidently distraught by all of this. Sarah so looked forward to seeing her again and being there for her to offer comfort in whatever situation she found. Sarah was thankful that Maria and Maggie had not only made the trek through Panama before her but that they had written her about their ordeal which was harrowing, to say the least. Their tale did not strike fear in Sarah's heart as well it could have, it only helped her to make better decisions in her own travels.

Dear Sarah,

At last, we are here in California. It is so good to be with my husband, James, again. The trip was very hard, but we are here safely, so I thank God for that. The journey from New York to Panama on the ship went pretty smoothly. However, the voyage from Panama to San Francisco was arduous as the ship was so overcrowded and dirty. The worst part of the trip, by far, was getting across Panama. Some terrible things happened there which frightened Maggie and me beyond belief, but thankfully all came out well.

When we alighted from the ship, many natives were waiting with mules for hire. The natives would then guide the travelers across the Isthmus. The problem was that there were so many people wanting to hire them that there were not enough to go around. There was a lot of pushing and shoving. I had Maggie and my two little ones and was not able to grab a mule. Luckily, after the crowd dispersed there was one last mule. I was able to get on the mule with the baby in my arms and little Mary Theresa behind me. This left Maggie to walk. I called out to her to keep up with me, and we would take turns riding. The mule had other ideas and forged ahead at a rapid pace trying to keep up with the others.

Maggie was left behind to trudge on by herself. At first, she was with a lot of other people who were forced to walk. She kept up at first, but got very tired and began to lag behind. The other people did not seem to realize that she was alone. She was confused by a false trail and taking it, found herself to be quite alone as night fell. She was lost, alone, stumbling along crying and calling out for someone to help her. She heard the hooves of a horse, and an Indian rode up to her. She knew she could not escape so waited to see what he would do. He took her by the hand and pointed off into the jungle. She was paralyzed by fear but followed him until they came upon a clearing where an Indian woman tended a fire by a grass hut. She was cooking. She spoke rapidly to Maggie in a language my sister could not understand, but she looked kind.

The woman took Maggie into the hut, placed some blankets on the floor and motioned Maggie to lie down. The woman then went out and brought back some food. Maggie was so hungry, she ate, then lay down on the blankets and slept a sleep of utter exhaustion. Sometime later, she felt herself being shaken awake. The woman led her outside where the man was mounted on a horse. He reached down and lifted her up in front of him. As they rode off into the darkness of the jungle, Maggie thought that she would surely die. They seemed to ride on for hours when they heard the hoof beats of another horse. Another Indian man rode up and a heated argument ensued. Maggie knew they were arguing about her. Some money exchanged hands; then Maggie was placed in front of the other Indian. The first Indian turned around and disappeared in the direction from which they had come.

Morning soon broke, and the Indian pointed ahead. Maggie could see water and a ship anchored upon it. This is where I caught sight of her and ran to meet her. There were many others who were waiting with me and we all started cheering.

I had met some friends on the ship who put up some money to hire the Indian to go in search of her. He had found her with the first Indian man and had to pay him to release her. Amazingly, several of the passengers persuaded the ship's captain to delay sailing, as they did not want to leave until Maggie had been found.

As you can see, Maggie had quite an adventure. She could not stop talking about it. I think I had a great adventure too, mostly worrying, but all is now well. I hope this finds you well. I miss you and Katie very much.

Your loving sister,
Maria

Sarah was grateful for this letter. Perhaps her sisters' experiences would help her make more informed choices.

The days flew by as the stagecoach plowed onward and they finally reached New York City. This metropolis was bustling. There were so many large buildings and crowds of people in a hurry, jostling each other, rushing to and fro. Noise escalated everywhere, and it did not seem to let up. For Sarah, used to the Indiana woods and a quiet tailor shop, it was overwhelming.

In spite of this, she was fascinated with everything she saw. She looked out on the many ships anchored on the Hudson and East River with intense interest. She wondered if the one that would take her to Panama was at anchor somewhere out there. An Irish relative of her brother-in-law, James O'Hara, owned a boarding house not too far from the docks. Sarah took a cab there, and they found a room for her. She did not spend any time sightseeing but made her mission a persistent pilgrimage to the docks and the ticket offices there each day. It did not take her long to finalize her trip.

It seemed that it was not too difficult for a steamship company to squeeze in a single small girl of seventeen especially in steerage class. She bought passage on the steamship Uncle Sam, sailing under the U.S. Mail line. It was scheduled to leave New York in two days, on February 5th. After crossing the Isthmus, she would meet her ship to San Francisco in Panama. It was the *S. S. Cortes* listed to the Babcock Independent Line. The fare for both ships came to over two hundred dollars, steerage all the way. It included an extra twenty dollars that Sarah realized was actually a bribe for "fitting her in at the last minute." Sarah briefly objected, but soon came to the conclusion that she had no choice. The fare was more than she had hoped to pay, but the fact that she only had to spend five days in New York was a blessing. James O'Hara's relatives were not charging her much for her room and board, but she knew some travelers waited a long time to book passage and this could seriously deplete your money.

After securing her ticket, Sarah carefully washed out her under things and the dress she had worn on the stagecoach. She meticulously mended every small rip and hoped this garment would withstand the rest of her journey. She kept her possessions to the minimum as she knew she had to carry her satchel a good part, if not all, of the way across the Isthmus. Her landlady gave her some tins of biscuits which she tucked in between her clothes. These, she thought, might become necessary for survival. She turned down the offered tinned meats as these weighed too much.

Once she was organized to leave, she found time on her hands. She chose to at least see some of the sights within walking distance. The waterfront along the Hudson and East River was colorful and in constant motion, with all of the ships arriving and departing. Sarah found this sight endlessly fascinating. One morning she walked all the way to Battery Park. This area came into being during the War of 1812. Although no ammunition was fired during that war, the place remained, and the fortification was named for the Governor of New York, DeWitt Clinton. New York City took over this facility from the army in 1823. She found Castle Clinton to be an imposing structure, its massive grey walls rising above her.

Since 1840 it had been used as an opera house and theater. Sarah walked around the walls. Finding an open door, she slipped inside. She could just make out through the gloom, an imposing stage and rows and rows of seats. She stood in awe as she realized that this was the very stage on which Jenny Lind, the Swedish Nightingale, had made her American debut just three years earlier. Sarah tried to imagine what that might have been like. She thought to herself that Jenny Lind's voice would have a hard time matching her sister, Katie's.

February 5th dawned bright and cold. Sarah ate a piece of corn-bread for breakfast, then gathered her shawl about her and picked up her satchel. Her landlady gave her a goodbye hug as she walked out the door. It was a long way to the dock, but Sarah trudged on, carrying her satchel.

I might as well get used to this, she thought. The first sight of the *Uncle Sam* made her heart race. *This is it! No turning back.* With her ticket in her hand, she made her way up the gangplank, carrying with her all of her earthly possessions including her precious treasures: her 16th birthday dress, her portrait wearing that dress, and her book of Plutarch's writings.

She was ready.

Sarah

February 1853

Panama

SARAH MADE HER way down to steerage. It was the lowest part of the ship, well below the water line. There were no portholes in the huge room to let in light. She stumbled over a multitude of people already there with their assortment of possessions. She found that the women and children were to be housed in one end of the room. There was a flimsy curtain strung across for minimal privacy. Miraculously she found a narrow bunk and promptly staked her claim on it by heaving her satchel onto it. She then took a look at her fellow passengers. Most of the women were simply dressed. Many of them either held infants or clutched toddlers to them. A few of the women were obviously drunk and dressed in garish, but tattered clothing. Sarah viewed them with dismay. Everyone crowded together, and already the smell of alcohol and unwashed bodies was overpowering.

One of the drunk women pushed her way over to Sarah. "Travelin' alone are ye? If ye're lookin' for work in Californeeay, I kin hep ye."

Pushing her flabby face close to Sarah's, she leered and chuckled a suggestive laugh. Her large breasts strained against her bodice and threatened to smother Sarah.

"No thank you," Sarah gasped, "I am going to be with my sister and her husband."

"Oh well, if that doesn't work out, remember me. Name of Dolly O'Neal." She lurched off down the narrow aisle. Sarah took a deep breath of the tainted air and let it out slowly.

Sarah made her way up the narrow stairs to the deck. Most of the passengers were now gathered on the decks waiting for the ship to embark. She did not have to wait long. The piercing whistle was soon followed by movement as the *Uncle Sam* pulled away from the dock. She ducked under the arm of a man whose rolls of fat strained against his suit.

He turned his pumpkin-shaped head her way and snarled, "Out of the way little girl!"

Sarah stood her ground and watched in awe as the city of New York gradually disappeared in the distance. The man waddled off, giving her a dirty look. She remained on deck for a long time. It was far better than the alternative of the oppressive steerage quarters even though it was cold. Sarah pulled her shawl tight around her and felt the wind sting her cheeks. She did not leave until the signal for dinner sounded.

The steerage passengers were served dinner "soup house style." Each lined up holding a pot or a mug into which was ladled the current fare. This first night it seemed to be a chicken stew with a piece of hard-tack on top and a cup of coffee. Sarah was hungry and ate greedily. It didn't taste bad at all. She was encouraged. However, sleep that night was another experience entirely. The passengers were excited at the prospect of at last heading to California. There was much loud talking and laughing especially from the male steerage passengers. Children, upset at trying to fall asleep on the lurching ship, cried continuously. Dolly and her friends were talking to the men and guffawing loudly. Sarah lay wide awake throughout the night, taking in all the many voices. Each of the nine days going south to Panama was much the same.

Sarah spent many hours on deck, catching glimpses of the shore-line when they sailed near it, watching miles and miles of unbroken ocean when not. She was fascinated with the seabirds and loved to see the gulls swooping at the ship and the pelicans diving for fish. The food was adequate and edible, and she learned to sleep a sleep of utter exhaustion in spite of the noise which had only grown worse with the addition of gambling and much drinking from smuggled flasks and bottles. She was thankful that she was able to adjust to unpleasant situations, but she looked forward to seeing Panama.

As the ship sailed south, the weather warmed up, finally becoming oppressively hot and humid. The steerage cabin with all of its human "heaters" became unbearable. Sarah spent even more and more time on deck, going below only when exhaustion overwhelmed her.

Early on February 14th, the *Uncle Sam* approached the port in Panama named Aspinwall. This port, later called Colon, had not been in use for long. William Henry Aspinwall started the United States Mail Line in 1848 to carry the mail from the east coast to California. The first port used in Panama was of Chagres, which, like San Juan del Norte in Nicaragua had a sandbar that required passengers to reach shore via canoe or native backs. Aspinwall claimed an adequate harbor and docks.

Sarah watched the ship approach the docks in eager anticipation. She carefully packed her satchel early. Clutching the strap, she watched the docking procedure with interest. Looking beyond, she saw a town that was in the raw growth period of a frontier habitation. Large warehouses rose near the dock, a scattering of small shops, hotels, and frame residences spread out from them. The streets were deep muddy tracks due to the daily rainfall.

William Henry Aspinwall and his partners started building a railroad across the Isthmus. In 1853 it was uncompleted, but a substantial distance of it was available for travel, which made traveling much more comfortable than the stagecoach, mule train, or on foot, as was previously required. However, Sarah was unable to afford the fare, so she did not even consider this option. She was against wasting any time here. She also steeled herself to resist getting sucked into the pushing, shoving contest that her sisters did to obtain a mule. There was only one thing Sarah intended to do, and that was to walk!

The way west was a muddy track with ruts cut deep by the wheels of the stagecoaches. Mule droppings covered the road. Soon Sarah's leather ankle boots were covered with a patina of brown. She looked down in disgust, then kept walking. Soon she noticed that the hem of her dress was coated with filth also. She hiked up her skirts to the top of her boots and marched on. Mosquitoes and horseflies buzzed about her neck and face and attached themselves to her exposed wrists and hands. She brushed them away with annoyed slaps, but they immediately returned to feast some more. Sweat ran down her face and stung her eyes. She swiped at her eyes with the sleeve of her dress and realized that traversing the Isthmus presented a real test of endurance.

Sarah was not alone on the trail. Many managed to rent mules and were plodding along. The stagecoach had not left Aspinwall yet, but she saw so many walking like herself, that she took some comfort in a shared trial. Occasionally, a snake would slither across the trail. Fellow travelers would call out a warning. Sarah was sure that some, but not all of these reptiles would be poisonous.

She noticed the enormous trees in the dense jungle. Everything was much bigger than she had expected. With the constant rain and heat, plants and trees grew to be giants. She passed under mahogany, chicle, strangler fig, guava and wild cashew. Ficus grew in abundance everywhere. She did not know their names but did recognize the many banana trees from the clusters of fruit. She did not know then that fruit would serve as the main part of her diet across Panama.

She heard movement in the trees above her. Looking up, she caught sight of shadowy forms leaping from branch to branch. Soon a green, slimy blob landed at her feet, then another. "Monkey droppings," a fellow walker commented.

She kept her head down to watch where she put her feet, but it really did not make much difference, the road was such a mucky mess.

The hours slid by, each much like the one before. Suddenly, out of nowhere, a huge black bird flapped down toward her. As it swooped at Sarah, she ducked and covered her head with her arms.

"That was a currasow," one of her fellow walkers commented.

"It looked like a creature from hell!" she exclaimed.

"It's a native species of Panama, and we will probably see more of them," her companion remarked. As predicted, more huge black birds flew over the pilgrims. Arms waved to ward them off and eventually they flew off.

"That was amazing!" Sarah cried. "I have never seen anything like it."

Sarah looked up immediately, forgetting the monkey droppings. She could see many other kinds of birds in the branches of the trees. Flashes of color caught her attention. "Oh my!" she cried in surprise.

"Wonderful, aren't they?" the man queried.

"Oh yes," she replied.

Pointing, the man said, "Look, over there. On that tree is a cinnamon woodpecker and just above it is another woodpecker, that one a red-crowned one."

Sarah looked carefully and saw the similarity and difference between the two birds. "You know your birds," she said admiringly.

"Yes. I do at that. My name is Henry Backman. I studied biology at New York University. My favorite subject is birds. I guess I could be called an ornithologist."

Sarah had never heard the term before, but she knew he meant the study of birds. Birds had always fascinated her. She remembered watching them around the log cabin in the Indiana woods. Now she saw so many colorful and varied kinds that she temporarily forgot the filthy mud, oppressive heat, and pesky insects. Henry Backman kept pointing out other kinds as they walked along. There was the slaty-tailed trogon, the hermit hummingbird, a toucan with a bi-color large beak, tanagers, and many other different kinds, each with its own vibrant color. There were crowds of noisy parrots, but the most spectacular of all was the scarlet macaws, huge birds painted with a veritable rainbow of colored feathers.

Sarah did not speak easily to strangers, and she would never have considered carrying on a conversation with a strange man in such an odd and challenging setting, but Mr. Backman was so interesting that she forgot all of her hesitations. He was middle-aged, with a brown beard, streaked with grey. Tall and somewhat stooped, he wore a battered straw hat on his head. A pair of wire-rimmed glasses perched on his crooked nose. He kept up a lively pace aided with a walking stick.

When they arrived at their campsite, it seemed the day had flown by. There were tents to rent and food for sale all at exorbitant prices. Sarah had eaten nothing since the early porridge breakfast on the ship. She opened her satchel and took out a tin of biscuits. Extracting three of the small morsels, she started to eat.

Soon a plump native woman came by and handed her two banan-as in exchange for a few coins. This was her supper. She spread her thin blanket on the muddy earth near a small family and pulled her shawl over her head. The heat made this almost unbearable, but it kept the insects from biting. Sarah was soon asleep.

Four days and nights were spent on the trail. Her thin blanket was caked with mud. The conditions and food were much the same. Sarah ate her biscuits and bananas with an occasional guava thrown in. At one camp the food offered for sale was a baked monkey. It looked to Sarah like a small burned child. She shuddered and was very thankful for her bananas and biscuits. On the third night, they encountered a lot of very sick people in the camp, unable to keep up on the trail. Many were shak-ing with chills or burning up with fever.

"Malaria," Mr. Backman said curtly. He immediately went off away into the jungle and came back with some bark stripped from a tree. He filled a pot with water and boiled it with the bark over the campfire.

When it had cooled some, he ladled it out to the sick travelers. "Cinchona bark," he explained, "better known as quinine. It will help control the fever. Unfortunately, they will have the disease for the rest of their lives. It will come back with all of the symptoms from time to time."

Sarah had nothing but admiration for her traveling companion's knowledge and just hoped she would not fall ill to this malaria or some other scourge.

The last night before their arrival in Panama City, they discovered a real tragedy at the camp. There was much sickness. Some had died. Brown skinned natives were digging graves. Several bodies lay together under improvised covers. To Sarah's dismay, she noticed that some of the mounds were very small.

"Panama fever," one of the travelers muttered. "Got 'em all." Sarah did not sleep much that night.

The last day was the hardest. Although only eighteen miles, they had to cross over a mountainous area. After descending on the other side they traversed a swamp with a road built across it. As Sarah walked on she could see what appeared to huge logs floating the water and along the shore. Some were moving. Crocodiles! They were frightening, and Sarah kept her eye on them in apprehension.

They reached Panama City at last.

Henry spoke to her as they walked into town. "I might stay here for a while and do some exploring around the jungle. There is so much to see. Then again, I might decide to go on to San Francisco. I haven't made up my mind yet."

Sarah felt a deep sense of disappointment. She had so enjoyed his company. "Well, Henry, whatever you decide, I wish you the best. Please do take care."

"You too, little miss. You are a brave one, and I am sure you will do well in California." He turned and strode off down the waterfront.

Sarah watched him until he disappeared, then looked around. This was a quaint walled town built many years before by the Spanish. There were narrow streets, balconied buildings, and even a large cathedral.

Many, many gold seekers were waiting to go to California and others, disappointed ones, were going the in the opposite direction. The travelers filled the streets and buildings. Sarah counted out her money and decided to rent a hotel room for the one night she would be here. She had to walk from one lodging house to another before finding a room she could afford.

She ate in a small café, ordering the cheapest thing on the menu, which was iguana stew. It was quite tasty. She spent the evening, bathing herself in a basin of water, applying ointment to her bites and blistered feet. She cleaned her skirt, blanket and shoes as best she could. She found that the leaves of the tropical bush outside her room worked wonders as cleaning material.

Sarah was grateful for a good night's sleep and awoke early. Her ship to California, the *S. S. Cortes* was waiting for her. Today, she would leave on the last leg of her trip.

Sarah

THE CORTES

IT WAS A huge, pushing mob that thronged onto the *Cortes*. Many had been awaiting a ship for a very long time. Ships had been delayed due to the quarantine for cholera in San Francisco Bay. Sarah was so grateful that she had been able to make timely connections. Now she faced a real problem. The steerage quarters swarmed with passengers. There was not a single bunk or hastily strung hammock available. Sarah climbed back up on deck to join the overflow crowd fighting for limited space. *This spot will have to do*, she said to herself and headed for an unclaimed corner and squeezed into it.

Word circulated that the ship carried twice as many passengers as usual. People boiled everywhere. Pushing and shoving, passengers fought for the rail to see the ship depart. Sarah gave up trying to get a view. She knew she would remember Panama City for the rest of her life without seeing it fade into the distance. She did not see anyone familiar from the trek across the Isthmus. Dolly had apparently decided to stay for the time being in Panama City. She looked in vain for Henry Backman, but did not find him. If he was on the ship, he was probably in first or second class quarters. Most likely, he had chosen to stay in Panama City.

The hot, humid air was suffocating, and shade was scarce. What shade there was became a source of contention as people pushed and shoved to get some relief from the blazing sun. The call for dinner created a minor stampede. Sarah held back and found herself near the end of the line. A stew of questionable content was ladled into her bowl and topped with a piece of bread. She noticed that the quantity was smaller than on the *Uncle Sam*. After the meager meal, the passengers lined up for a small helping of plum duff and some watery coffee. Sarah ate hungrily. Her tinned biscuits were gone. She had tried to ration them in the trip across Panama, but they, with the bananas, were all she had to eat. It would be fine with her if she never saw another banana for the rest of her life.

Sleeping that night was difficult with so many crowded together. Even at night, it was sweltering. Each of her breaths was labored. Sarah spent her time looking up at the stars which seemed so much more brilliant out here than back in Indiana. It made her realize how strange her life had become, to be out here on the ocean, trying to sleep in the midst of this mass of humanity. She thought that there was a distinct possibility that it might become more stranger yet.

A small dollop of lumpy porridge was served in the early morning with more watery coffee. Sarah had to use the latrine down in steerage and found it already foul with overuse. She was relieved to come back up on deck where at least there was a slight breeze. At noon the hungry passengers were served only a couple of biscuits each. Dinner was another stew made with dried beef. If anything, there was even less than the night before, and there was no plum duff.

Sarah was so tired that as soon as it was dark, she drifted off to sleep in her cramped corner. Many of the passengers started drinking and gambling to pass away the hours. Sarah managed to sleep through the noise until she woke with a start. One of the male passengers was singing in a loud, clear voice. She listened to the words:

The greatest imposition that the public ever saw,
Are the California steamships that run to Panama;
They're a perfect set of robbers and accomplish their designs
By a general invitation of the people to the mines. . .

This rendition brought forth a round of whoops and guffaws and requests to teach the song to the surrounding crowd. The singer affably agreed, and soon Sarah was treated to a whole choir singing the words. She wished she had a paper and pencil to write this down, however they sang it so many times that she was sure she would remember it forever.

The second full day at sea, Sarah was pulled from her ocean-swept reverie to hear loud, anxious shouts. "Fire, fire!" came the cry.

Smoke billowed below decks, from the vicinity of the paddle wheels. Soon they could see flames. Some of the passengers started to panic and rush for the stairs. Sarah stayed where she was and held fast to the rail. In the rush and confusion, she had no idea what was going on. Although she told herself to stay calm, she felt a panicky sensation in her stomach. Her heart beat rapidly. Would they all die here on their way to California? There had been other disasters with ships. Some never made it to California.

Finally, the flames subsided, then the smoke. People stopped running about so much, and Sarah allowed herself to take a deep breath. Word eventually circulated among the passengers that the fire had destroyed one of the two paddle wheels, but the other one had survived, and they were proceeding with that one doing the work of two.

The mood of the passengers was gloomy. One of the passengers, who happened to be a Protestant minister, organized a church service to pray for safe passage. Sarah hung on the edges and listened to the words of exhortation and prayers the minister offered. They seemed to calm and comfort many of the passengers. Sarah, still confused about her faith, also found this helpful and appreciated the minister's efforts.

The ship put in at Acapulco. Usually, the stop was to take on more passengers who had managed the route across Mexico. The *Cortes* could hold no more bodies. The sailors did load on some supplies, including fresh fruit, which was a welcome treat, but the hungry people consumed it all in short order.

The shortage of food soon became dire. It was evident that the ship had not stocked enough to feed double number of passengers. The three scant meals were cut down to two, then just one a day. That one, served in the late afternoon, day after day, was the notorious meal of the gold rush, *lobscouse*, the same concoction of salt pork, potatoes and hard tack that Ann and her family ate on the *Lewis*. Word got around that the food was being rationed, but it had already become obvious.

There was sickness on board, mostly from Panama fever and just plain dysentery from the crowding and dirty conditions. The rank smelling water was rationed as well. It was dark and filled with strange floating film. One by one, some of the sick died. Their bodies were quietly slipped into the waters of the Pacific Ocean along with their hopes and dreams.

Murmuring among the passengers increased. "What is going to happen?" muttered a swarthy man at the rail.

"God only knows! This ship is in real trouble," growled another.

"Might sink at any minute!" spat a third man.

Comments flew back and forth. Suddenly a shout came from the front of the ship. "Meeting to be held aft! All to attend the meeting!"

This announcement threw a hush over the crowd, and the passengers surged forward.

Captain Cropper appeared before the crowd. His face had a gray cast, his eyes bloodshot and his uniform wrinkled and smudged with soot. He pulled himself up straight and shouted, "The situation with the ship is serious. We have only one wheel and a shortage of food. We could put in at San Diego, and you can disembark there."

Murmuring among the passengers increased to a low roar. Soon arguing and shouting ensued. Several women started crying. Their children, seeing their mothers' distress, took up the chorus.

"I just want off this tub!" shouted the swarthy man. "It's going to sink for sure!"

"But how would we get to San Francisco?" another queried.

"We don't have any more money to pay for a trip from San Diego to San Francisco," sobbed a small woman with several children hanging onto her.

I don't have any money for that trip either, thought Sarah. *What in the world will I do?*

"Let's take a vote!" came a hoarse voice from the back.

"Yes, yes, a vote, a vote," several took up the cry.

A vote was duly taken, and the majority agreed to continue on to San Francisco. Sarah breathed a sigh of relief.

Several days passed before the last night on the miserable tub arrived. The food had finally run out two days before. Sarah was agonizingly hungry. She was also shivering with the bitter chill. Sarah had at first welcomed the cooler weather as they steamed north, but as it grew colder, keeping warm became more difficult. Wrapping herself in her shawl and dirty blanket had not been enough. She was shivering, but she could not suppress the excitement she felt. Tomorrow they would be in San Francisco.

It seemed that her fellow passengers were excited about this too. Few slept, and the boisterous talking and raucous singing kept up until almost morning. She listened to the songs and upon hearing one of them, had to laugh to herself:

We lived like hogs penned up to fat,

Our vessel was so small,

We had a 'duff' but once a month,

And twice a day a squall;

A meeting now and then was held,

Which kicked up quite a stink.
The captain damned us fore and aft,
And wished the box would sink.
We sobered off, set sail again,
On short allowance of course,

With water thick as Castor oil,
And stinking beef much worse;
We had the scurvy, and the itch,
And any amount of lice.
The medicine chest went overboard
With blue mass, cards, and dice.
Each verse was followed by a rollicking chorus:
Oh, I remember well the lies they used to tell,
Of gold so bright it hurt the sight,
And made the miners yell.

This song, and many others like it, were sung over and over. Sarah wondered what some of the eager pilgrims back east would think if they heard these as they waited to go to California to "make their fortune."

Sarah was more than ready to leave the stinking ship the next day at the Embarcadero in San Francisco. She walked down the gangplank, weak from hunger, sunburned and dirty. She planted her feet firmly on the wooden boards. It was only then that she realized the date: March 5th, her eighteenth birthday! She smiled.

Happy birthday, Sarah, she whispered.

San Francisco

$\mathscr{Ann}$

January - August 1853

Earthquakes and Other Experiences

THE BEDRAGGLED SEXTON and Fithian families huddled on the Embarcadero after straggling down the ramp from the Lewis. They gathered the children and their baggage together. Richard spotted a horse car coming toward them. "This way," he beckoned. They wearily climbed aboard and found seats. "Does this car go to Bush and Sansom Streets?" Richard queried the driver.

"Indeed it does" was the reply.

"We're headed to the Rasette Hotel," Richard announced. He had researched the different hotels available and had settled on this one.

The horse car took off, and before long they reached their destination. Ann wondered what the desk clerk thought about their sorry condition but then concluded that other guests had surely been as unsavory at times. Still, it hurt her pride. Rooms were available, and soon they began to settle in. Ann felt the first order should be a good soaking bath for each one of her family including herself. Hair was washed and fresh clothes unpacked and put on. Ann bundled up the smelly garments and put them out in the hall. She swore she would burn them, but her frugal nature took over.

She gave them to a Chinese man who had a laundry nearby. The desk clerk had recommended his services highly, "Chang Yung will get them clean if anyone can!"

Unfortunately, Chang Yung appeared the next day with many apologies, "Could not get smell out. Many washings, no get out."

"Well, I tried," Ann thought. She paid the man for his efforts.

The families ate their meals in the hotel dining room. The food was good. No *lobscouse* appeared, and Ann hoped she would never see that dish again as long as she lived.

The hotel was a rather sedate, quiet place compared to several other San Francisco hotels–including the El Dorado, the Verandah, the Bella Union, and the Empire–which all allowed gambling. The Americans patronized these dens at night and the Mexicans during the day. Favorite games were faro and craps. Myriads of French women had come to San Francisco to work in these places. Men paid an ounce of gold (around $16) for one of the women to sit with them at their table. They paid more for "extra services" after hours. Often there were brawls in the gambling dens and much bloodshed. Still, lawlessness was not as bad now as in previous years. In 1851 a vigilance committee was formed. Two Australian gangs, The Hounds and The Sydney Ducks practically took over the city. The vigilance committee rounded up the gangs. Several ringleaders were hanged, and many were banished. The vigilance committee disbanded shortly after this.

Richard seemed to get his energy back almost immediately, as did the children. All of them were ready to explore their new world except Ann. It took her several days to feel like wandering out to see the city. She was utterly exhausted by the journey. The older boys and Richard found something to do every day, so one day she took Lewis and Elizabeth and boarded a horse car to see her new home. The day they arrived Ann had stared in amazement at the hundreds of abandoned ships in San Francisco Bay. They were an eye-sore in an otherwise beautiful setting.

The place was starting to resemble a real city. Gone was the ramshackle canvas and lean-to jungle so evident at the beginning of the Gold Rush.

Six fires had torn through San Francisco in the last few years. Now, more permanent buildings were being built. While the streets were still muddy tracks, some effort was put into maintaining them. Not only were there horse cars evident, but there were heavily loaded wagons everywhere, piled with hay, lumber or other supplies pulled by draft horses. Many sported a four-in-hand team.

Crowds of people milled on the streets. Different ethnic groups converged or mingled with others. There were the Chinese, Mexicans, Chileans, French, English, Scots, and in spite of the recent gang problems, Australians. Various languages and accents of English could be heard in abundance. It was easy to pick out the prospectors from the gold fields because of their rough apparel. Flashily dressed women from the hotels and the Barbary Coast flounced about and stood in doorways. Ann also noticed there were some families, and even single women, modestly dressed, which reassured her that San Francisco was becoming more civilized.

All of the children, except baby Lewis, were enrolled in the recently organized school much to the three eldest's disgust, as they would have much rather been exploring this fascinating place. The Rasette's Chinese cook, Kuo Lee, packed lunches for them to take each day. Richard was unusually quiet about his future plans. This made Ann uneasy.

She took a deep breath and blurted, "Are we to stay in San Francisco? Will we move to a mining camp?"

Richard rubbed his chin. "I'm looking into all the possibilities," he replied. His answer did not reassure her.

She knew that he spent every day out talking to prospectors, mining suppliers, and other businessmen. He was keeping a journal on what he found out. She tried to be patient, but it was hard.

There was a daily newspaper called the *Alta California* and Ann eagerly read it every morning. It listed ships arriving with the names of their passengers. Ann wondered if anyone she had known back in Ohio was there. It only listed the last name and initial unless the person died en route, then their hometown was posted. So many died, she noted, and their dreams died with them. They died of Panama (Yellow) Fever, malaria, typhoid or cholera. Each time she read about these, she thanked God for the safe passage of her family.

In February she read that a Reverend William Speer had opened a mission house for the Chinese and had been a missionary in Canton. The news pleased her. Entering the kitchen, she stated to Kuo Lee, "It is good that this missionary teacher is telling thy people of God and Jesus Christ."

Kuo Lee snorted, "No good! Chinese Buddhist. No Christian."

She did not bring up the subject again.

On February 22nd, there was quite a celebration with a parade and bands. It was the second anniversary of the founding of the San Francisco Fire Department and also Washington's birthday.

On March 1st, the floor lurched under her, and she grabbed at a chair to steady herself. The other chairs in the room started sliding. A clutch of fear grasped her. It must be an earthquake! She had heard about them, but this was a new experience. She prayed for the jolting to stop. When the shaking subsided, she slowly let out her breath. She did not like it one bit, but it would not be the last quake she experienced. By the time the Sextons moved on from San Francisco seven months later, there would be over thirty more.

March brought some other important happenings. In the bay, there was a new lighthouse on Alcatraz Island. If one looked carefully, one could see it in the daytime; however, it could not be seen at night until later when the revolving lantern arrived from France.

March brought Richard's decision; about their *near* future at least. After talking to many people who were from the gold fields, Richard decided that mining for gold would be way too risky for a man with a family. Several thousand prospectors had already filed on the best placer claims. Ever the businessman, he knew that more money could be made in another direction. He told Ann that he wanted to purchase a coal and wood yard which had was already well established. It had a small frame house next to it on Union Street close to Dupont. He took Ann to see it. The business was neat and well kept up, and the owner was selling for health reasons. The house was a disappointment, really no more than a shack, but Ann thought she could make it into a home even if they were crowded. The purchase was finalized, and the Sextons moved out of the hotel. Ann spent the next weeks cleaning, making curtains and putting in a vegetable garden. She was happy to do her own cooking after so long a time. Lewis was a toddler now and into everything. Ann wrote long letters home describing her new life.

Ann continued to read the *Alta California* avidly. She was shocked to learn that the ship they had arrived on, the *Lewis* had run aground and sunk off Bolinas Bay on April 9th. *Good riddance,* she thought. *At least it won't be killing off more people with its terrible conditions.* She was so thankful that all the passengers made it to shore.

Fire still occurred in San Francisco in spite of its much-touted fire department. On April 25th, the wharf near Drumm Street burned with a loss of $22,000. The same day another on Stockton Street near Union was lost to the tune of $20,000. Ann worried about fire in the coal and wood yard and their small wooden house. She was extra careful with the stove and saw that the chimney was cleaned on a regular basis.

In May there was much excitement upon the arrival of the Countess of Landsfeldt, more popularly known as Lola Montez. She would be performing at the American Theater in The School for Scandal. Ann read about this exotic creature, but no way would she be going to see the play, nor would her family. She was a good Quaker still, and this was very worldly. When sometime later, Lola performed her notorious "Spider Dance," she knew for sure she had been right.

Another phenomenon appeared in August. Handbills were post-ed everywhere that the "head of the notorious bandit, Joaquin Murieta would be on display at a local saloon." Ann's boys saw this and ran for the house, bursting in they begged, "Please, Mama, can we go see the bandit's head?" Jumping up and down, they continued to plead, "Oh please, please!"

"No, thou may not go! This is nothing for young boys to see."

They sneaked out to go and see the grisly sight anyway, and when Ann caught them, they were severely punished.

The boys otherwise thoroughly enjoyed their summer vacation from school. They were out exploring every minute. Ann gave up trying to ride herd on them, but would admonish them as they left to "Please, please be careful!" She was glad when they became engrossed in a new occupation. Ships from Chile had been arriving all winter and into the spring with loads of fruit. The boys collected the discarded peach pits from the streets and brought them home. There, they were added to a bag of apple seed which had traveled from Ohio with them. The apple seeds were reputed to be descended from trees planted by Johnny Appleseed himself in Ohio. "Good work, boys," Richard praised them. "We will plant these when we start our nursery."

A nursery? Ann thought. *Is this to be the next project?* With Richard she never knew.

Sarah

MARCH–AUGUST 1853

ANOTHER TAILOR SHOP

MARCH 5, 1853, Sarah's eighteenth birthday, found her standing on The Embarcadero in San Francisco, California, her destination. She faced a dilemma. Clutched in her hand was a small scrap of paper with the address of the O'Hara family. She had so many questions. Did her sisters, Maria and Maggie, still live there or had the family moved on? Was Maria still alive? She had been so sick, that was the reason Sarah had made this long trip. And the last question, how was she going to get to their home to find answers?

Sarah knew the address was near Mission Dolores. Many Irish families had settled in that neighborhood and attended Catholic services at the mission. However, she did not know how to find this mission district. To top everything off, she was out of money. There was no way to hire a horse and carriage or even ride the horse car. *Well, first things first,* she thought. Walking up to a wharf worker, she asked directions to Mission Dolores. With that firmly in her head, she made the next decision. She had walked across the entire Isthmus of Panama; she could surely walk a few miles to Maria's home.

Clutching her small tapestry bag, the gift from Miryam Hirsch, she set out. She soon found out that the hills of San Francisco were a lot steeper than those in Panama. She also had not allowed for her malnourished condition. The lack of food on the ship had sapped her energy and forced her to stop and rest often.

During one of these walks she sat dejectedly on a low wall. A freight wagon stopped in front of her and a shaggy, bearded man leaned down, "Little miss, where are you headed? You look plumb knackered."

Sarah was wary of over-friendly men, but this one's face looked kind. "I am headed to my sister and brother-in-law's home near Mission Dolores," she replied.

"Well, it just so happens I have to deliver this lumber pretty near there. Why don't you climb up here? I'll give you a ride."

Gratefully, Sarah accepted his invitation, and with a sigh of relief, rode for most of the remaining miles.

The kind man dropped her off just a half mile from her destination. As she walked the final distance, fear gripped her. *Would they still be here? What if Maria had died of her illness?* Sarah dreaded this possibility, and her heart started beating wildly. She finally found the cottage she was looking for. She knocked tentatively on the door. There was no response. She knocked again more loudly. She heard steps, and the door flew open. There stood her younger sister, Maggie. She had grown so tall–and looking like a young woman.

"Oh, Maggie," she gasped.

Maggie did not recognize her sister at first, then screamed, "Sarah, Sarah, Sarah! Is it really you?"

Sarah grabbed Maggie and pulled her into a tight hug.

Then Sarah heard running steps and looking over her shoulder to see Maria rushing up she gasped, "Oh, Maria, you're alive!"

"I am indeed. I cannot believe it is really you, Sarah!"

There were many more hugs, kisses and freely flowing tears as the sisters reunited at last. Maria and Maggie were there alone with little

Mary Theresa. Sadly, Maria's little baby boy had died of diphtheria the year before. James was away on one of his sales trips to the gold camps.

The next few weeks were a time of reunion and rejoicing as the sisters caught up on all the news. Sarah was able to rest and heal. Maria cooked her nourishing meals, and Sarah relished every bite. As time passed, however, Sarah knew she had to make some decisions. She was sleeping on a pallet on the pine board floor. She did not mind this, and it was comfortable enough, but James O'Hara was expected home momentarily. The cottage was crowded now, and when he arrived, it would be even more so. Also, Sarah was penniless. She was unable to contribute even one cent to the household expenses.

She remembered Isaac Hirsch's recommendation that she look up his friend and fellow tailor, Elias Goldman, here in San Francisco. Isaac had actually written a letter to his friend telling him that Sarah was a very experienced and talented tailor herself. She made plans to see Herr Goldman. She just hoped he needed an assistant. If he had a place for her to room and board there, that would be even better. She would not only free up space in the O'Hara household but be able to help them out financially.

The next day, Sarah put on her best dress, carefully arranged her fine brown hair and set out to find the Goldman tailor shop. Maria insisted that she take some coins for the fare on a horse car, so Sarah did not have to walk all the way to Sacramento Street where the tailor shop was located.

She found it with no trouble. On the window in gold letters were: "Elias Goldman, Schneider." Underneath was written, "Fine tailoring for discriminating ladies and gentlemen."

Sarah was impressed. The place looked prosperous. She opened the door, bells rang in the back, and a stooped older man came out. A tape measure hung around his neck and a pin cushion strapped to his wrist. His hair and beard were white.

Seeing this fair-haired *shiksa* in his shop, he said in accented English, "May I help you?"

Sarah replied, *"Shalom Aleichem,* Herr Goldman."

Taken aback at the Yiddish greeting, Elias replied, *"Aleichem Shalom!"*

Sarah then explained in Yiddish who she was and produced her letter from Isaac Hirsch.

"Ah yes, dear Isaac. He is a very good friend. We are from the same village in Bavaria. If he says you are a good tailor, I believe him, and yes, I could do with an assistant who is not afraid to work hard. The last one was lazy. I had to fire him. When can you start?"

"Right away," Sarah answered. "I am staying at my sister's home near Mission Dolores." She did not venture to ask if there might be room and board involved.

"*Oy vai,* that will never do. You would tire out traveling back and forth to work. Isaac said you lived with his family and he thought of you as a tochter—*a daughter.* My wife, Rebecca, and I have a small room here where the umzitztiger fresser—*free loader stayed.* You are welcome to stay here."

Sarah could not believe her ears. It was all working out so beautifully. She was even more convinced when Elias quoted her a salary. Together with the room and board, it was very generous. *Business must be good,* she thought.

Sarah appeared the next day with her small satchel of possessions. Elias introduced her to his wife, Rebecca. Tall and thin with dark hair, mixed with grey, she was the exact opposite of Miryam Hirsch with her roly-poly figure and easy laugh. Rebecca did not seem given to hugs like Miryam either, but as time went by, Sarah found in Rebecca's shy, quiet demeanor, a gentle, loving heart. Sarah was glad down the road that she did not judge her that first day they met. Rebecca towered over her short, stooped husband. Together, they made quite a pair, however Sarah noticed that they seemed to be devoted to each other. They had married young and had four grown children. Two who lived nearby and two who had moved to distant places.

The room she was to live in was tiny but very neat and cozy. She unpacked her few belongings and reported for work. Elias seemed pleased with the tasks she completed for him that day. Sarah shared dinner with them, and the familiar, delicious Jewish food made her feel right at home. She wondered if all Jewish women were as good cooks as Miryam and Rebecca.

The days flew by, Sarah settled into a routine. She loved the tailoring work, and Elias praised her freely and often. This made her feel warm all over, not only from the blush that lit her cheeks but somewhere around her heart. On her day off, she went to see her sisters. Sometimes she accompanied them to mass at Mission Dolores, but she did not go to confession or take communion. She sought the companionship with her sisters more than a religious experience.

She occasionally went with the Goldmans to temple. While she enjoyed the singing of the cantor and the ceremony, she knew she was not a part of it. Sometimes, as to faith, Sarah felt she was a wanderer and an outsider. The thought would fleetingly pass through her mind, *Would she ever find a faith she could accept wholeheartedly?*

One day, as Sarah was walking up Sacramento street, she noticed a man walking ahead of her. He looked familiar, but she wasn't sure. She quickened her pace and sneaked a peek at him from the side. She could not believe her eyes. "Henry Backman, is that really you?"

Henry turned toward her, surprise and delight flashing over his face. "Sarah, Sarah, what a great day this is! I am actually seeing you again. What have you been doing and how was your trip to San Francisco?"

"Oh Henry, the trip was awful. We ran out of food and nearly starved, but I arrived in one piece. My sister has recovered, although her baby died. I am working for a tailor just down the street. What about you? Did you find any more birds in the jungle?"

"Oh, yes, it was a good time for exploration there, but after a few weeks, I felt I needed to move on. I got on a ship, and it was pretty terrible also, but we did make it, and here I am. I am teaching at the new school that started up here. I enjoy the students, and I think I might stay for a while." They made arrangements to meet for a meal sometime soon.

Sarah did not read the local newspaper every day as did Ann, but one did not need a newspaper to note the earthquakes. The first one scared Sarah. It was so unpredictable, and she wondered if it would ever end, but as they seemed to occur on a regular basis, she soon came to take them in stride.

Sometimes news came to the shop with its customers, and she would listen. Early on, she heard that a steamer had exploded on April 11th with a considerable loss of life. It was not one on the Panama run, as the ship had been on the bay between Alviso, near San Jose to San Francisco. It caught Sarah's attention because its name was the *Jenny Lind*. Sarah remembered staring at the stage at Castle Clinton in New York City where the real Jenny Lind had sung her first American concert.

Sarah felt sorry for the victims in the explosion. Not only were there many who died, but also scores who were scalded by steam. She heard that often the captains of these ships wagered against each other and a race would take place. Many a ship's boiler exploded when pushed beyond its limit. Rage filled Sarah's thoughts as she concluded that this must be what happened. All of those poor people hurt and killed because of the greed of two men!

One day, not long after Sarah started working at the tailor shop, a man came in looking around expectantly.

"Is Elias Goldman here?" he asked in heavily accented English.

"He's in the back. I'll fetch him," Sarah answered.

The man was relatively young with dark brown hair and a beard. When Sarah brought Elias to the front of the shop, the two men looked at each other in amazement, then proceeded to hug one another ecstatically, talking excitedly in Yiddish.

After a while, Elias backed away and wiping his eyes with the back of his hand, exclaimed. "Sarah, please meet my friend, Levi Strauss. He arrived last month from New York, but before that he was from my village, Battenheim, in Bavaria. Our families go way back together as does that of Isaac Hirsch. Sarah lived and apprenticed for two years with Isaac in Fort Wayne, and she speaks fluent Yiddish. You'll never believe it; she sounds like one of us!" Sarah shook Mr. Strauss' hand.

The conversation continued, and Sarah learned that Mr. Strauss, his brother-in-law, David Stern, and his wife, Fanny, who was Levi's sister, had arrived in San Francisco the day after Sarah on the *S.S. Tennessee*. The *Tennessee* later sank just outside the bay. All of the passengers were saved, but it was a frightening experience for everyone. Levi and Sarah shared their experiences during their nightmare trips from Panama to San Francisco. Sarah later wrote to the Hirsch's about meeting their old friend.

Levi Strauss came into the shop on a regular basis after that. He told them that he and David Stern would be opening a dry goods store just up Sacramento Street from the tailor shop. He planned among other things to make tents for the miners in the gold fields. His brother, Jonas, would ship the material to him from New York City where Levi had spent the last six years. He seemed so full of optimism and good spirits that Sarah always looked forward to his visits. Moreover, she felt a real bond with someone who had arrived the day after she had in this strange new land.

The months passed. By the end of August, Sarah came to realize that her life was about to change again. James O'Hara wanted to move his family north to the Sacramento area, possibly even up to Sutter County. There he would be closer to his market for the picks and shovels he sold to the miners. Maria and Maggie were putting pressure on Sarah to come with them. She knew that soon it would be decision time.

Ann and Sarah

September - October 1853

A Meeting

ANN KNEW A change was coming. The Sexton family would most likely be leaving San Francisco in the next few months. The coal and wood yard was turning quite a profit. Richard and his crew ran it efficiently, but again Richard was restless.

Ephraim Fithian was planning to move his family to a tiny settlement called Ione up in Amador County on the edge of the Mother Lode. Richard had taken a trip with Ephraim to look over Ione where he found some land that he thought might make an ideal plant nursery. He felt that there would be a growing demand for trees and plants for the new farms that were going in all over California and he had put a down payment on the property. He planned to put to good use the fruit pits and apple seeds he had stored away.

Ann knew a move was coming. She remembered how much Richard had disliked running the farm back in Ohio, but he always had an interest in growing things. The six months in San Francisco had brought in money they had salted away. The yard went up for sale.

In the meantime, life had to go on. School would be starting soon. Ann noticed with dismay that the three older boys' trousers were sadly in need of replacing. Summer activities had worn holes in knees and ripped seats. Mending would not repair the damage it seemed. the boys had grown so over the summer, and all of their pants were too short, even their Sunday best. Ann made inquiries of her neighbor as to her recommendation of a good tailor. They need both school pants and dress pants she said.

Mrs. Mitchell did not have to think for long. "Oh, do go to a tailor on Sacramento Street named Elias Goldman. He's Jewish, of course, but he does an excellent job, and he's reasonable."

One morning, as the sun pushed through the fog, Ann herded her boys onto a horse car and headed for Sacramento Street. As she pushed open the door, she was greeted by a young girl with a pale face and light brown hair. "Good morning, may I help you?" the girl asked.

Ann noted that she spoke unaccented English. I do not think she is Jewish, she thought. "Yes," Ann replied. "My boys are in need of trousers, two pairs each. I hear that the quality of Mr. Goldman's work is excellent. That is why I am here."

Sarah gazed back at this unusual sight. Here was a small, thin woman with a narrow face, dressed in a plain grey dress with a Quaker bonnet on her head. Beside her were three stair-step boys, who were having a hard time standing still and seemed uncomfortable to be here.

"I can certainly help you right now. I will take their measurements, and then you can pick out the material you want. We have several samples from which to choose. I am sure you will want something that wears well. I can make suggestions in that regard."

Ann seemed uncertain. This girl could not be out of her teens, probably nearer William's age. Did she know what she was doing? "Isn't Mr. Goldman here. Doesn't he do all that?"

Sarah smiled. "Mr. Goldman is out of the shop this morning on business. If you insist on him doing the measuring, you would have to come back, but I can assure you that I know what I am doing. I am a full-fledged tailor, having apprenticed back in Fort Wayne, Indiana for two years with a friend of Mr. Goldman's. Here, I am the assistant tailor."

Ann thought it over. It would be a real trial to shepherd the boys back here. Today had been bad enough, rounding them up and bringing them here. "That will be fine if thou do it. Please go ahead with the measuring."

Sarah brought her notebook, pencil and measuring tape and proceeded to measure William, Joseph, and George Sexton, much to their extreme embarrassment. Ann then looked over the swatches and agreed with Sarah's recommendations as to durability. These garments would have to last a while, she reasoned. There probably would not be an opportunity for quality clothing up in Ione.

Ann was impressed with this young girl's confidence and dexterity. She thought for a moment and in spite of her hesitation as to its propriety, asked, "How old are thou and when and how did thou come to California?" Sarah blushed and hesitated. *Oh no,* thought Ann, *I've offended her.*

However, Sarah then looked directly at this unusual woman and replied. "I arrived here on March 5th this year. It was my eighteenth birthday."

Ann was impressed with her forthrightness. "Is thy family here too?" she queried.

"My oldest sister and her husband were here already with my younger sister. I came out alone because my older sister was very sick. She's much better now. We were all from the Fort Wayne, Indiana area."

Sarah could not believe she was giving all of these personal facts to this stranger, but she was compelled to answer her questions fully and honestly.

"Thou came out alone?" Ann was incredulous, "I was with my husband and five children. My youngest was only six months old when we started out from Ohio. We were from the Cincinnati area. That is not all that far away from where thou are from. How did thou travel?"

Sarah sighed, "I walked across Panama."

Ann found this amazing. "We came across Nicaragua, mostly by boat, only the last part was on mules."

Ann then related her frightening experience when she thought she had lost two of her sons.

While the two were talking, the boys were just outside the door waiting and getting more and more restless. "I must go. When will the trousers be ready for me to pick up?"

"By the end of the week," Sarah replied.

"Good, I'll be here and without my ruffians."

Sarah thought for a minute, "Perhaps you can stay a while and have some tea then."

"I'd like that," smiled Ann.

As the odd little woman sailed out the door and gathered up her brood, Sarah wondered why she had ever invited her for tea. She just did not do things like that. Picky social amenities bored her, but she was strangely drawn to Ann Sexton–Mrs. Richard Sexton–she read from the order slip. She found herself looking forward to her return.

Elias was in and out on various errands all week. Sarah herself stitched up the trousers for the Sexton boys. She looked forward to Ann's return, and sure enough, on Friday morning Ann walked in the door alone. Sarah brought out the pants. Ann inspected the workmanship and pronounced approval. "They're very well made. They ought to last, but my boys can be hard on clothes."

Sarah laughed. "Oh, I'm sure they are, but this is good fabric, and I stitched them carefully."

Ann looked up in surprise. "Thou made these thyself?"

"Oh, yes. Mr. Goldman has been busy, and I knew you needed them right away."

"Well, thou did a beautiful job."

Sarah felt a glow of pride, then remembered her promise. "Let's have that tea."

Sarah hung a "Be Back At" sign on the door and led Ann into the living quarters. Hannah was busy in the kitchen, and Sarah introduced her to Ann. Politely, she asked if she could make some tea.

"Oh, let me do it," Rebecca said. "And I have some strudel just out of the oven."

"Thank you so much, Rebecca. That would be wonderful!"

Over tea, the two women, Ann and Sarah, picked up their conversation from last time. Each shared their horrifying experiences on the ships from Central America to San Francisco, telling tales of dirt, sickness, bad food, and hunger. They laughed as both pronounced they never again would eat *lobscouse*. Sarah added bananas to the list from her steady diet of them on her "walk" across Panama.

"I wish we could do this again," Ann said, "but it looks as if my family is moving to the hills. My husband is buying land in a town called Ione up in Amador County. He wants to start a nursery."

Sarah sighed, "I too am leaving San Francisco soon. I am going with my sister's family either to Sacramento or Marysville.

"Well, I do wish you the very best," Ann smiled. "You are a courageous young woman."

Sarah smiled back. "Thank you for saying that. You also are a brave woman. I only had myself to worry about. You had all of those children!" The two briefly embraced, and Ann walked out the door.

On her way home to the small frame house, Ann suddenly thought back to the time when she had been Sarah's age. She was just getting ready to marry Richard. She remembered the comparison game they played with each other when they bragged about their noble ancestry to each other, each trying to top the other. She then thought of this lone Irish girl from humble beginnings and murmured. "Courage is courage. It does not matter in the least who thy ancestors were, noble, good, bad.

It's what thou does, the choices thou make, the hardships thou endure in this rough and savage new land."

She wondered if she would ever see Sarah again.

The Settling

YOUNG RILEY BISBEE IN NEW YORK BEFORE LEAVING FOR CALIFORNIA

Sarah Malone and Riley Bisbee on their wedding day,
Sacramento, California, July 4, 1854

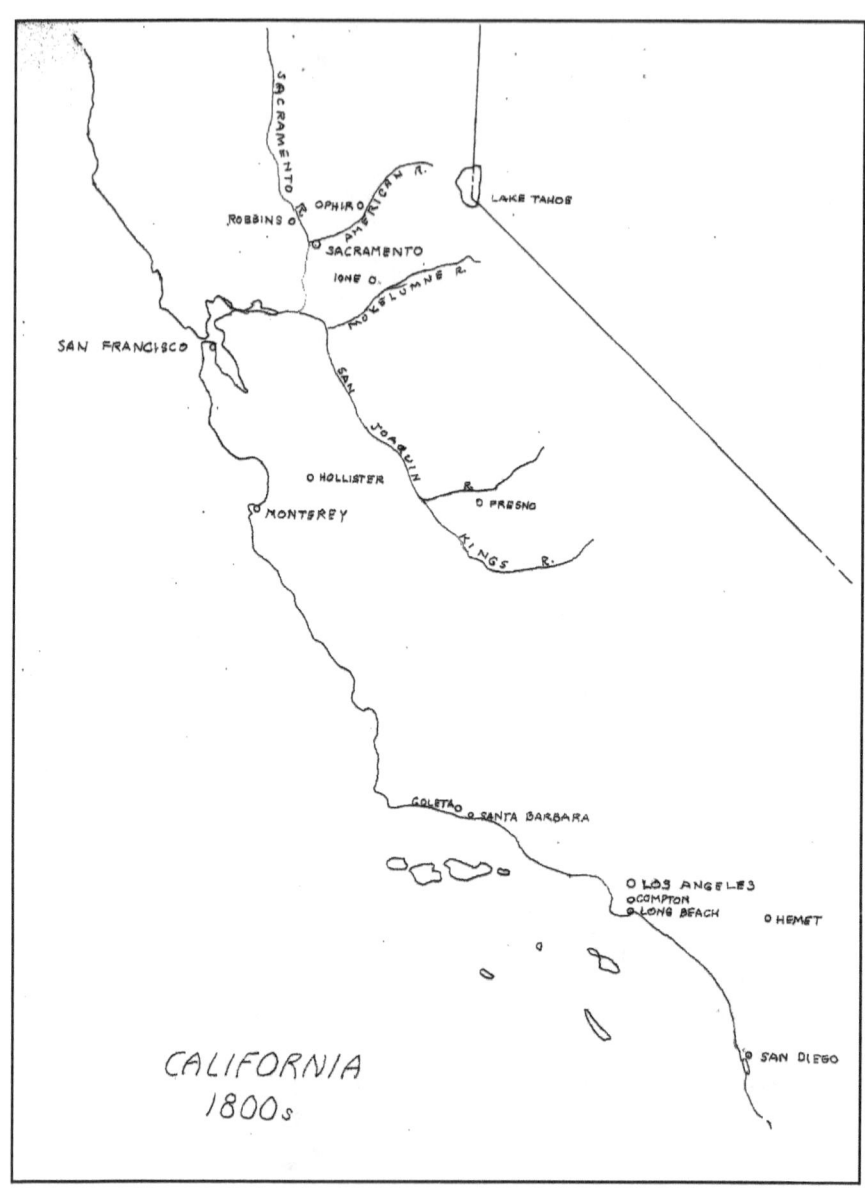

CALIFORNIA 1800's

1853-1854

A WEDDING IN SACRAMENTO

IN MID-OCTOBER, THE O'Hara's, together with Maggie and Sarah Malone boarded a steamer to Sacramento. As they made their way up the Sacramento River. Sarah could not help but think that this ship and its short journey was a far cry from her last two voyages. Once they arrived in Sacramento, it did not take long to locate an adequate house for rent on the edge of town. Maria was quite happy with this arrangement as it would allow James to be home with his family more often than in San Francisco. Sarah and Maggie were less enthused.

Like San Francisco, Sacramento had been plagued with fire. A massive one, just a year before, burned eighty-five percent of the town. Rebuilding was taking place, but it was slow. The city fathers decided that the way to go to prevent more fires in the future was to build with brick. Some buildings were completed, but many still in progress. Even with this, the town possessed more of a rough mining camp aura than San Francisco, which was on its way to becoming a city of distinction.

Sarah felt she needed to find work. She did not want to become a burden to her sister and brother-in-law. She started her work search with visits to the few tailors in town, but there were no openings. Some suggested she open her own business either as a seamstress or tailor, but she had no money to rent a shop, and the O'Hara house was too out of the way for a business location. By chance, one day she heard that a small hotel near downtown was looking for a cook. Sarah had been cooking since she was a little girl. She could produce a meal with no problem. She had no training in haute cuisine, but this small, rowdy, hostelry did not have that kind of clientele. They just wanted plain, everyday, good food. The innkeeper who interviewed her thought she would do just fine and hired her.

Sarah walked to work each day through the muddy streets. The hotel furnished the basics to the hoard of miners in town from their diggings. They would arrive dirty and disheveled, looking forward to a bath, a real bed, and a simple home-cooked meal. Sarah was good at providing the latter. She never minded the roughness of the men, their boisterous laughter or their teasing. She was pleased when some would praise her cooking. A few weeks after starting work, one of the waitresses quit. Sarah recommended Maggie for the job. Maggie was sixteen years old now and a lovely young lady. She learned to serve the food in a very short time.

On Maggie's second day of work, Sarah walked out of the kitchen just as she heard a panicked shriek. She saw Maggie near a table of miners with a shocked look on her face. One of the miners had his hand on her sister's backside and had apparently just pinched her. Sarah, picking up a full pitcher of water off the nearby stand, walked determinedly over to the table, and poured the whole thing over the miner. Gasping and sputtering, the miner let go of Maggie.

"There will be no more of that, Charlie! " Sarah snapped. "If you try it again, the next dousing will be hot coffee! And that goes for any of the rest of you!"

No more dousings were necessary. The men behaved themselves.

James came home for Christmas, and the little family was able to have a small celebration in the rented house. Maggie and Sarah with their salaries and Maggie's tips managed to buy modest gifts for everyone, even a doll baby for little Mary Theresa. Maria cooked a tasty meal, and they all sat down at the table, thankful for being together in this most unlikely place. Sarah missed Katie and only wished she could be here with them.

One day in early March, Sarah realized that it was her nineteenth birthday. She thought, *How very much had happened in this last year!*

Maria gave her some of her beautiful handkerchiefs she had e embroidered, and Maggie produced a simple bead bracelet she had strung together. Sarah was touched.

That day two young brothers came into the hotel dining room. They were slender, with tousled brown hair and the same dark, piercing eyes. In sharp contrast to the majority of the boisterous diners, they seemed very quiet, which caused Sarah to take notice. She wondered if they were just stopping by for the night. By their soiled and rough clothing, she could tell that they had just come from the gold fields. She was surprised when they showed up the next night, all cleaned up and respectable. She was curious as to what their story might be.

The two young men stayed at the hotel for two weeks. Sarah learned that their names were Riley and Orsamus Bisbee. They had arrived in California from New York State two years before. They were attempting to make their fortune at mining but came up mostly with disappointment. Occasionally Sarah had spoken to them casually, and in time, she could not help notice that Orsamus was very taken with Maggie. Sarah's protective nature toward her sister put her on alert, but Orsamus was always the gentleman. She came to the conclusion that the brothers had had a good upbringing. The pair soon found rooms in town but went into the hotel often for a meal. They praised Sarah's cooking until she blushed.

In April, Sacramento was surprised by another fire. While this one did not do the damage of the 1852 fire, it still managed to burn several blocks in the downtown area, including the courthouse. Sarah and

Maggie were at work when the alarm sounded. They were forced to flee the hotel as for a time it looked as if the fire would consume it too, but fortunately, with the help of the fledgling fire department, the fire was stopped, and the small inn survived.

One day, Sarah was taken completely by surprise when the quieter older brother, Riley, asked if he could call on her and meet her family. She was speechless. She had not even noticed him paying her any particular attention.

She sputtered as she answered, "I'll let you know about that."

"I'll be back for your answer tomorrow," Riley replied.

Sarah fled to the kitchen. "Oh my, oh my, what do I do now?" she gasped. As she and Maggie walked home, Sarah told her about Riley's surprise question.

"Wonderful!" was Maggie's response. "They are so very nice. I am happy for you."

"But I haven't decided what to do yet," Sarah blurted. "Maybe I don't want to do this."

"Oh, Sarah, don't be silly. All he wants is to call on you."

Sarah did not sleep much that night. Over and over in her mind flew all of the assumptions that she had formed about her future. She remembered what Da had said about her being plain and needing more training to support herself because she might never marry. Riley's asking to call on her meant he was interested in her, maybe even wanted to court her. The situation was something she had never anticipated. Did she really want to even think in this direction? She was torn.

At breakfast, Maria brought up the subject as Maggie had told her all about it. "What are you going to do, Sarah?"

"I'm not sure yet," Sarah replied.

"Oh, Sarah, what do you have to lose? Maggie says they are really nice young men, well brought up and all. If you do not like him after getting to know him better, you don't have to keep on seeing him."

"But, he's a miner, Maria. If you are honest, there isn't a future in that. All of the good gold strikes have already been found."

Maggie, who had just come in for breakfast broke in, "Oh Sarah, didn't you know? They are buying some land up in Sutter County. They're going to farm that land together."

Sarah paused. No, she did not know this. "Well, I guess it would not hurt to let him come calling. Then you can look him over too," she said to Maria. "I trust your judgment."

That evening, when Riley came into the dining room, he looked very nervous. As Sarah approached his table, he looked up. "What is your decision?"

"It is all right with me if you come to call," she said hurriedly and turned to go back to the kitchen.

"And where may I find your home," he asked.

Sarah half turned toward him, gave hurried directions and added, "You may come by on Sunday afternoon. It is my day off."

So their courtship began, shyly at first, sitting in Maria's parlor, getting to know one another. Riley had perfect manners. He was quite intelligent and well read. He came from an old family that traced its lineage back to the "First Comers," which were those sailing to America on the Mayflower. This impressed Sarah. Sometimes they took short walks together. Riley would tell her about his dream of farming up on the Sacramento River near the tiny town of Robbins in Sutter County. He grew up on a farm and knew how it worked. Riley seemed very interested that Sarah knew so much about raising crops and caring for livestock. He already knew she was an excellent cook.

As time went on, Riley seemed ever more taken with her. One day in early June he approached her with a determined look in his intense eyes. He asked her to marry him and go to live with him on his farm. The proposal did not come as a surprise to Sarah. While she was not madly in love with him, she had come to have a deep affection for Riley and respect for his ambition and intelligence. She suspected that Riley had determined to find himself a wife before attempting his farming project. He would need the help, and with her background, she filled the bill. Still, she loved children and wanted a family. There might never be another chance. Perversely, she thought about Da and smiled. I'll show him!

She turned to Riley and said, "Yes, I will marry you."

He bent to kiss her for the first time.

Sarah's sisters were ecstatic about a wedding, but Sarah insisted that it be simple. Since she was not associated with a church and it did not matter to Riley, they agreed to be married by a judge on the Fourth of July. The courthouse had burned down in April, so the ceremony took place in the Sacramento City Hall and Waterworks before a Judge Landrum. Maria was Sarah's matron of honor, Maggie her bridesmaid and Orsamus, the best man. Sarah could not help noticing the looks that flew between the latter and Maggie. They guaranteed another wedding in the near future.

ANN CLAYPOOLE SEXTON

RICHARD SEXTON

Ann

October - March 1853-1854

Bedbug

TWO WEEKS AFTER Sarah made her way up the Sacramento River by steamer, the Sexton family, all seven of them, rode the same ship. However, Sacramento was not their final destination. After leaving the ship at Sutter's Landing, they took a Wells Fargo Stagecoach to the town of Ione. The stagecoach drivers whipped their horses mightily in order to make the trip in the shortest time. The ride was rough in the extreme, and family members were jounced around unmercifully. It was with great relief that Ann spotted the two hills standing as sentinels above the town. The wagon train hurtled its way between Indian Hill and Dutschke Hill, and Ann caught the first glimpse of her new home.

The town of Ione is in Amador County. It is in the foothills of the Sierra Nevada, in the middle of the Mother Lode. In 1853, it claimed about one-hundred-fifty residents. Three of those were the Fithians: Ann's sister Hannah, her husband Ephraim, and their daughter Matilda, who had arrived in there two months earlier.

Ann looked forward to seeing her beloved sister but felt some apprehension about this new town. Upon arriving in Ione, Ann learned that the town had only recently been christened with its poetic name. Before that, it had been called Bedbug. Ann was thankful for the name change as she could not even think of what her family back in Ohio would think if she wrote them that she now lived in Bedbug. She wondered if this former name denoted the town's most prolific inhabitants.

The family made their way to their new property on the edge of town. It was located on Sutter Creek, named for the man who had panned for gold in its waters. Ann surveyed the brush-covered field and shabby lean-to which was to be their new home

Richard squeezed her arm and said into her ear, "I promise to build a better house. It will be my first project."

Ann settled her family into their new, but crowded home and set about unpacking. The surrounding hills were just greening up with the beginning of the seasonal rainfall. They were covered with oak, digger pines and manzanita. The level expanse of their property on the creek was covered with sagebrush and manzanita, but the air was clear and the sky a brilliant blue. The town consisted of only a few dilapidated buildings facing a dirt street. However, the people living there seemed friendly enough.

True to his word, Richard's began to build them a more adequate house. Ephraim and the older boys pitched in, and soon Ann had a rough, but livable place for her family. The next job was to clear and prepare the land for Richard's proposed nursery. This endeavor was hampered by the increasing rains that came in December and January. Richard's mood was as gloomy as the weather. He was a doer, and all of the inactivity weighed heavily on him.

Finally, in late February and early March he was able to attack the property. It took much back-breaking work, but the boys we a big help. Surprising to Ann, both William and Joseph seemed fascinated with the proposed nursery project. Ann had to take this as compensation for the lack of educational opportunities in the tiny settlement. The school had just opened its doors the year before and only went through eighth-grade.

She also longed for a Quaker meeting house, but there was none. She contented herself with reading her Bible and the writings of George Fox. Often Hannah joined her, and after their silent prayers, they would have tea and talk about old times. The company of her sister made up for a lot.

In the spring, Ann dug and planted a vegetable garden in the hard clay soil. She thought of the last one next to the shack near the coal and wood yard in San Francisco, and she wondered how long they would stay here before Richard, with his restless spirit, would want to move on. She at least hoped she would see her neat rows of beans, squash, and cabbage produce food for her table.

Richard had his ground ready for planting in early spring. It was with much enthusiasm that the Chilean peach pits and Ohio apple seeds were put into the earth. He carefully painted a sign and put it up by the road into their property. *Sexton Nursery and Fruit Farm* stood out in black letters on a smooth pine board. Richard was proud of his efforts.

Ann's garden started to come up as did the nursery plants. The days turned warm. Sunshine with occasional showers made for a lovely spring. The boys were so excited when the peaches pushed green tendrils through the moist earth. Richard felt the same way about the apple sprouts. Every member of the family made a daily pilgrimage to the plot to inspect their progress. Something about spring and its time of renewal gave Ann real hope for the future.

One night, Ann awoke when it was still dark. It was cold in the house. The days had been so warm they had only used the stove for cooking. She got up and pulled extra covers over the children and a quilt over herself and Richard. She did not think much of this at first, but as she dozed off again, warm in her bed, her eyes flew open, and her heart sank. It was really cold! This could not be a good thing.

Sure enough, the next morning as they arose, they could see the rime of a heavy frost over everything. Richard pulled on his clothes and went out to inspect the tree shoots and other plants. Ann soon followed.

Her garden had survived for the most part, with only the edges burned by the frost. Some of Richard's plants had also made it, but all of the tiny peach and apple trees were a total loss. Shriveled and brown, they looked like the dead things they were. As Ann glanced at her big boys who had worked so hard to gather these, she could see the gleam of tears in their eyes. She thought of the hope Richard had carried with him all the way from Ohio in that bag of apple seeds.

The disappointment was something to be taken in stride, so when Richard vowed to try again next year Ann pulled that comment close to her heart. At least he was planning to stay another year. It seemed that late frosts were often the case up in the foothills. Ann heard that before the town was named Ione, or even Bedbug, it had been called Freeze Out!

$\mathscr{S}arah$

1861-1862

THE FLOOD

SARAH SAT BACK in her rocking chair and heaved a tired sigh. It had been a long and busy day, and the constant downpour did not help. She was weary, and she had not yet prepared for Christmas which was fast approaching. Baby Ada was only three weeks old, so Sarah had not regained her strength fully from the delivery. This newest addition to the Bisbee household busily nursed at Sarah's breast. Sarah caressed the soft down on her tiny head and gave a silent thanks for yet another healthy child. Her mind flew back to the beginning of her present life.

After her marriage to Riley in Sacramento, they moved a few miles up to the tiny town of Robbins in Sutter County. Riley owned land along with his brother Orsamus on the Sacramento River near where the Feather joined it. Together, the brothers had one hundred forty acres next to the river. Some of it was covered with tules, but even though the land near the river was inundated at times when the river retreated, the topsoil was rich beyond belief.

Riley built a small cabin in late fall, but all summer they had been living in a tent. Both of them had worked from daybreak to dark, on the cabin and clearing the land. Sarah was used to hard work, so she took this in stride. The early days of California was no place for lazy people.

The following spring there were crops to plant and a vegetable garden to put in. Sarah admired her hard-working husband and held a real affection for him. Riley treated her with respect and even admiration. She treasured his pride in her.

The year flew by. The couple's first anniversary was celebrated with a bouquet of wildflowers presented to Sarah by Riley together with a big hug as he whispered in her ear, "It has been a good year, my girl."

A few weeks later, Sarah realized that she was going to have a baby. They had been so busy that she had not even thought of the possibility, but when she was sure, she happily told Riley. He was elated. Sarah always wanted to have children. She looked forward to the event eagerly. She purchased soft flannel yardage in town and in the evenings by the glow of the lantern, she skillfully made small wrappers, nightgowns and blankets. After finishing these, she made another trip to town and bought pastel embroidery floss and embroidered tiny flowers and vines on each garment.

Early that March, Sarah sent Riley to fetch the midwife. Late that night, a tiny boy baby arrived. They named him Chauncey Burrell Bisbee after Riley's mother whose maiden name had been Chloe Burrell. Baby Chauncey's head was covered with an abundance of dark hair, which Sarah stroked lovingly as she inspected his small body. He was absolutely perfect and seemed quite healthy. Sarah rejoiced in this wonderful gift.

A year and a half later, a little girl arrived in the household, Almira Augusta, promptly nicknamed Allie. Two years went by before another tiny addition made her way home, Emma Minetta, with the same dark hair of her brother, Chauncey.

Now here was tiny Ada Marrilla, exactly two years younger than Emma. Sarah thought that she was indeed blessed. Her children were healthy and beautiful. Riley was a hard-working husband and an attentive father. She could not ask for more.

Baby Ada finished nursing and Sarah put her on her shoulder and gently rubbed her back until the tiny bubble came up along with a mouthful of milk. How Sarah loved this time, everything so quiet except the rain beating on the roof. It had been raining all day, and the children had been restless indoors. She savored the quiet as they slept. She gently laid the baby in her cradle and poured herself a cup of tea.

She would have a few moments to herself before joining Riley in their big bed. The rain hit the roof in torrents now. The downpour raised a small worry in Sarah's mind. She thought back to the time of the flood in Indiana. She was just a small child, but she remembered it vividly. Da had hired a couple of men to help with some of the work around the small farm. Like now, it had rained all day.

When Da got home, he remarked that the river had risen to reach the second fence rail between the cabin and the river. Everyone was tired, so they went to bed, but in the middle of the night Da let his arm drop over the side of the bed and found the floor covered with water. He woke everyone up. The men picked up the children, and Sarah found herself clinging to a broad back as they were carried up the hill to a neighbor's place. The water continued to rise and almost reached this place too, but not quite. Sarah had an unsettling memory of the neighbor's cow going to the edge of the water to get a drink and being swept away. The children cried, and the cow struggled but was soon gone.

She remembered how they watched other animals, houses, furniture, churns, and anything that would float being carried away. When the water receded, the cabin was in ruins. The bag of flour was a solid mass of dough, the sugar and salt supply dissolved in sticky puddles, the bedding wet and muddy. Sarah remembered that she and the other children had made a tent out of quilts and sheets. They all thought this was a big adventure. If the present rain does not stop, Sarah thought, this could be a flood like the one in her childhood, only she would not find it such a great adventure this time.

Thinking of her childhood brought thoughts of her sisters. Maria's husband, James O'Hara, had died of pneumonia, leaving Maria a widow with a small daughter. A few years later Maria married Joseph Lambert and now had twin daughters. As Sarah predicted, her sister, Maggie, married Orsamus and was her neighbor. She had two daughters, Flora and Eva. Her sister, Katie, still lived in Urbana, Illinois. She was married to her minister, the Reverend Reasoner and had a son, Matthew. Sarah had not seen her since leaving Indiana, although they wrote each other often.

After finishing her tea, Sarah put out the lantern and peered out the window, hoping to see if the river had risen, but it was so dark and wet that she could not see much. She quietly undressed and pulled her flannel nightgown over her head. She slipped into bed exhausted and fell quickly asleep. It seemed that she had just drifted off when she was shaken awake. Riley stood over the bed. "The river's up and rising rapidly. We don't have much time. Get the children up and dressed, we need to get to higher ground."

Sarah was on her feet in an instant.

Going to her children's beds, she shook them awake and said to each, "Up, up, up. The river is coming. We have to leave."

She tossed their clothes to Chauncey and Allie, five and four, and pulled two-year-old Emma's dress over her head. Stuffing their arms into coats, she pushed them out the door after Riley. Hastily throwing on her own clothes, she grabbed baby Ada and wrapped her warmly. Putting diapers into a bag, she was out the door a few seconds after the children.

The water was at the house, and it was rising Riley hitched the horses to the wagon, and as the family climbed in, he called, "Giddap, Let's go!"

They clutched the sides of the wagon as it lurched forward following the road to higher ground. They found their way through the dark with the rain pouring down on them. Sarah stretched a tarpaulin over the children. Allie held baby Ada on her lap. Sarah, sitting on the seat by Riley, was soaked to the skin. When they reached higher ground, they found a number of their neighbors there. Maggie and Orsamus had pitched a shelter of sorts, and the family crowded in with them. Sarah struggled to keep the children dry and tried to dry out her own soaked clothing. It was a miserable night, but as the first light came at dawn, the sorry group could see that not only had the rain stopped, but the water was receding.

The refugee families made their way back to their homes by mid-day but were discouraged to find utter devastation on their return. Sarah thought back to the destruction of her home in Indiana so many years ago. This time it was even worse. Miners had been dredging up in Marysville on the Yuba River. Their digging and disturbance of the river had raised up tons of muck and debris that with the flood, had found its way down the Yuba, to the Feather, to the Sacramento and brought massive destruction with it. Their home was full of sand, dirt, and trash. Even worse was the thick layer of sand covering the previously rich farmland making it impossible to grow anything in the future.

Riley and Sarah salvaged everything they could from their home and loaded it in the wagon. The contented life Sarah had known for over seven years was over, their future uncertain. They needed to find shelter for the family. They headed to Sacramento which had also flooded. Maria and her husband lived there. The Bisbees arrived on their doorstep seeking shelter. Maria took in the bedraggled family and fitted them in as best she could. Christmas was a sorry celebration that year, but the family gathered, little knowing that the worst was yet to come.

Less than two week later, on January 5th, 1862, the warm rains came again in torrents. The abnormally large snow-pack in the Sierras melted, and the rivers raged. Sacramento was flooded and stayed that way for days on end. The Lambert and Bisbee families found refuge on the second floor of the house, but before it was over, they ran out of food. Everyone was hungry. There were no levees on the Sacramento River at that time. Water stretched everywhere. Farms were destroyed for hundreds of miles. Thousands of animals drowned and those that made it to higher ground starved to death. A three-hundred-sixty mile lake covered the length of Central California.

Looking out at the scene, Riley muttered. "I'm getting out of this valley for good. We're going to the hills!"

Sarah

1862 - 1869

OPHIR

RILEY WANTED TO move up into the hills after the flood waters subsided, but the family had no money. They lost everything on the ranch near Robbins in the floods of December and January. All they owned when the waters subsided were the clothes they had on at the time and the horses and wagon they rode in to Sacramento. They were fortunate that Riley was able to get the outfit to higher ground when the second flood hit while they were staying at Maria's.

Riley's anger at the recent catastrophe frightened Sarah. He flew into a rage at the slightest provocation. Sarah and the children learned to tiptoe around him. His fury would then dive into a deep depression where he would sit and brood for hours on end, then stomp out of the house not telling her where he was headed. Sarah suspected he was drinking but did not question him. He seemed like a stranger to her, and she missed the old Riley desperately.

One day, he came home in a better mood. "I think I have a way to earn some money."

"How's that, husband?" Sarah queried.

"There seems to be a big need for drayage up into the hills. Many goods need to be hauled, and if you're lucky, you can pick up a load going back and make the trip really worthwhile."

Riley seemed taken with this idea and Sarah, to encourage him, said, "If this is true, it would be something you could do. We still have the wagon and good horses too. Where did you hear about this?"

He looked at her, a wary expression on his face, "Oh, just around, talking to some men." he replied evasively.

Sarah suspected Riley had heard it in a tavern but did not pursue it.

Riley set out to look for work in the teamster business and soon had his first load to haul up into the mountains. More work came quickly. The load going up was usually mining equipment and machinery, coming down, lumber. The weeks sped by. Sarah found it hard living with the Lamberts. With two families in the house, it was crowded. There were six children to be fed and cared for, and baby Ada often cried all night with colic. With a stoic determination, Sarah had faced a lot of changes and disappointments in her life. Each time she had taken each one as it came, but this time, she felt defeated.

The loss of her home and everything she and Riley had worked for was devastating. Living in crowded conditions where nerves were tested and tempers flared was a burden. The confusion and fussiness of the children added another stress, especially a crying infant who robbed sleep. Then there was Riley, a man she felt she never really knew. Frustrated and discouraged, Sarah was ashamed to admit that his long trips on the road were a relief of sorts.

One day, when she felt she would scream if she stayed in the house one more minute, Sarah found Maria in the kitchen. "Would you watch the children for a bit? I want to take a walk. I feel about to explode, and I think this would help"

"Yes, I will watch them for a while, but please try to be back for

Ada's next feeding. I don't need a crying infant on top of everything else."

Sarah pushed back the quick clench of guilt she felt. She had to get out!

Once out in the welcome sunshine, she realized that it was Sunday morning. Her feet took her up H Street where she soon came to a Methodist Church. She heard singing coming from inside. She recognized it to be a hymn, but it was unfamiliar to her. She had been without a church for so long. Disenchanted with her experiences in the Catholic church of her childhood and rejecting a conversion to the Jewish faith, she deliberately avoided any association with religion. Now, she stood outside this place of worship and felt drawn to go inside. Sarah stepped hesitantly into the foyer of the church, then peeked into the sanctuary. A number of people sat in the pews dressed in their best clothes. They sang earnestly if not harmoniously. She entered through the door and slipped into a pew in the back. The minister, a Dr. W. S. Urmy, strode up to the pulpit as the Amen was sung and asked the congregation to bow in prayer. Sarah sank her chin onto her chest and listened. It was a simple prayer for God's grace and enlightenment. The sermon that followed was eloquent, but powerful, explaining God's love and forgiveness through His son, Jesus Christ.

Sarah was moved. She questioned if some of her trials were God's way of reaching out to her, telling her she needed something or someone to lean and rely on besides herself. She was tired. She was discouraged. She just needed to do something. At the end of the sermon, Sarah expected Dr. Urmy to give an invitation to come forward and give herself to God, to accept Jesus Christ as her Savior. She had heard about these "altar calls" and the ensuing emotional meltdown. But Dr. Urmy did not. Instead, he merely bowed his head and prayed for those hurting in the congregation, that they might know God's unconditional love. Sarah could not help herself. Invitation or not, she was on her feet and walking to the prayer rail. Dr. Urmy came to meet her and took her hand. He held it while the congregation sang a final hymn and departed. Then he knelt down with Sarah and spoke with her gently until she fully understood that this was what she wanted in her life. They prayed together, and when Sarah walked out into the sunshine, she felt as if a thousand pounds were lifted from her back.

During one of Riley's trips up into the mountains, he came across the town of Ophir. It was the largest town in Placer County at the time, and the location was in a little valley surrounded by lush green hills. It was cut through by the Auburn Ravine and near this Riley found forty acres for sale at a reasonable price. It was beautifully rich farmland, and Riley knew he had found their new home. The wagon runs had paid well, and he worked without even a day off for several months. He approached the owner, a Mr. McColier, with a sizable down payment and a promise to pay it off in two year's time. The owner, anxious himself to relocate, accepted Riley's proposal and the deal was closed. When Riley came down the hill, he burst into the Lambert house shouting for Sarah. "I found it! We now have a new place to go to up in the hills," he exclaimed.

Sarah was speechless. She couldn't believe it. The old Riley come back to life and with the promise of a home of their own again

Finally, she found her voice. "Oh Riley, I am so happy. God answered my prayers."

Riley looked at her intently. She was a different Sarah. She never talked about God or praying before.

It was a gorgeous spring day when the Bisbee family left Sacramento and moved to Ophir. Sarah delighted in the beauty of the little valley and the surrounding hills covered with trees. Auburn Ravine cradled a lovely creek filled with trout and even salmon fighting their way upstream. The ranch came with a house and some outbuildings. The owner even left some of his furniture which was a blessing to the bereft family. The land had been in use for crops, and there was a pretty little apple orchard. Riley planted hay as well as corn, potatoes and pumpkins. They had good neighbors who Sarah got to know. The Winters family owned a ranch on the south side, the Curts on the west and the Hendons on the east. There seemed to be a real sense of community in the little valley; people were friendly and helpful. After the isolation on the ranch on the Sacramento, Sarah welcomed this, but she missed having her sisters close.

Sarah now knew she needed to be in a church to find the uplifting inspiration and fellowship she craved. There was no Methodist Church in town, and she did not want to attend another Protestant denomination after her positive experience at the church in Sacramento, so she bided her time. Her prayers were answered when several Cornish families in the area, staunch Methodists, formed a small house church. They met in different homes, sang the good old Methodist hymns, sometimes with a home organ accompaniment or sometimes *a cappella*. They read from the Bible and prayed together, then had refreshments. When the small group grew large enough, they asked for a visiting preacher to come their way on a regular basis. They wrote a letter to the district superintendent of the Methodist Episcopal Church requesting this. When the answer came, they were elated. The Reverend Duke soon visited them once a month and preached a resounding sermon each time.

Civil war raged in the east during the Bisbee's stay in Ophir. News filtered in, and Sarah felt a great sorrow hearing of the awful toll in human lives on both sides. *War is so wrong*, she thought, *brothers fighting brothers*.

The little house church prayed constantly for those both in the conflict and the families who lost loved ones. Several young men from Ophir came together and traveled east to enlist in the Union Army. When one of them, Joshua Long, was killed at Antietam, the war truly came home.

Progress also came to the little mountain town. The Emigrant Trail wended its way over the Sierras very near to the now dubbed Bisbee Ranch. It had seen the migration west over many years. In 1865, service was put through to Auburn by the Central Pacific Railway. It too ran close to the Bisbee's home. Its co-founder, Leland Stanford had a store in nearby Auburn and could be seen from time to time visiting there.

Sarah still possessed a vast thirst for knowledge. She had soaked it in while she was at school and even when that was cut short, she found the library at the Hirsch's. She read and read for her entire two years there. For the short time she lived at the tailor's in San Francisco, she devoured that small library. She loved history, especially ancient history and archaeology. She often wrote essays, if only for herself, practicing the proper use of the English language. She loved words with a passion and absorbed new ones, adding to her vocabulary. Fortunately, during the time in Ophir, she found that some of the inhabitants owned books which they willingly lent to her. Each time, she felt she had discovered buried treasure.

The children, were for the most part, healthy, save for the usual childhood maladies which Sarah nursed them through lovingly. They were growing, and they were beautiful to her. She was surprised to discover in the fall of 1865 that she would be adding a fifth child to the family. Her pregnancy was easy, and in May she delivered another son, Frederick Clarence. She felt content and truly blessed. She gave thanks to God.

Riley was her only worry. He worked hard on the ranch always accompanied by his dog, Max. He seemed for periods of time to be content if not entirely happy and treated the family well. Then the sour moods arose when nothing suited him. Sarah noted that Max, the dog, was the only one he tolerated at those times. Riley would become critical of her, and the children irritated him. Sarah took care of disciplining the children. Corporal punishment was accepted as routine and Sarah employed a small switch from one of the fruit trees which she applied to small legs when there was sassing or disobedience. But during this time, she was dismayed when Riley would explode in a rage at one of the children, taking off his belt and whaling at them. What struck fear into her was that often he did not know when to stop and the recipient ended up with angry red stripes on his or her legs. She found this hard to either understand or tolerate. When he was in one of his moods, he shouted not only at the children but at her as well. She suspected he was drinking again. He did not seem to do this at home, but she smelled it on him sometimes when he returned from town.

As 1869 arrived, Riley brought up the subject of moving once again. Sarah was not sure exactly how she felt about that.

$\mathscr{A}nn$

1855-1864

A LYNCHING

RICHARD, TRUE TO his word, planted the remaining Chilean peach pits and Ohio apple seeds the next spring. The family was optimistic of a good result and an emerging orchard of trees. Again, a late frost hit. The sprouts turned brown, and Richard vowed that from then on he would use budded stock.

Ione was a staging area for the miners in that part of the Mother Lode. The town was often inundated with loud, rough men in dirty clothing, looking for a bath and strong drink. The taverns and saloons thrived. Usually, a pair of miners faced off over real or imagined slight and a fist-fight would ensue. Sometimes, more inebriated men would join in, and the fight spilled into the dusty main street.

When Ann ventured into town for a newspaper or supplies, she tried to avoid the sources of mayhem. She did not always succeed, having to flee to the other side of the street to get out of the way as a chair or a body came flying out of a doorway. Richard held no such compunctions and sought out those who had just returned from their claims in the hills. There remained in Richard, the niggling attraction of gold. At one point, he ventured forth himself into the hills during the nursery's offseason. He had some success and continued this practice for a few years, but finally concluded that more money could be made in business than in mining.

The nursery thrived and became a source of plants and trees for the locals, both for the homesteads and the farms. They planted a huge vegetable garden every year. The yield from this and later from the fruit trees that began to bear apples, peaches, and plums were in heavy demand by the miners. Added to this were chickens and eggs. Richard established a delivery system, loading up the wagons and taking supplies to the miners. The men were willing to pay the going exorbitant rates, so the Sexton family profited mightily. Richard was soon able to start a small money lending business which also filled the family coffers.

The whole family worked hard. Ann took charge of the chickens, feeding and cleaning the pens, gathering and washing the eggs, and butchering the old hens when they no longer produced eggs. She helped in the vegetable patch with weeding, gathering, watering and harvesting. Along with all this, Ann canned and preserved the fruit and vegetables for their family's use. She felt a sense of pride when she stood back at season's end to admire the colorful jars of beans, tomatoes, pickled beets and corn relish. She thought to herself that their bright colors and varied shapes would even make a good painting. When winter set in, the family always enjoyed eating her creations.

Ann loved her children with an open heart. She was proud of all of them. They were growing up strong and healthy. Both William and Joseph worked hard in the nursery. They were fascinated with horticulture and wanted to learn as much as they could about it. Ann was thankful that with their education cut short by the lack of schooling in the area, they were able to learn this useful skill. Often out on the road on their own, Ann trusted their good judgment to keep them safe.

One day, Joseph stumbled into the kitchen late in the afternoon. Richard was sitting at the table reading the newspaper as Ann worked at the soapstone sink. Joseph, white as a sheet, gasped for breath.

"What in the world is the matter, son?" Ann asked, grasping Joseph's arm and leading him to a chair. "Are thou all right? What happened? Please tell me!" she beseeched. Joseph tried to catch his breath.

"Ma, Pa, it was awful!" he gasped.

"What was, for heaven's sake!" Richard snapped.

Finally, Joseph calmed down enough to be coherent, "I was in the wagon coming back from the mining camp after delivering the eggs and vegetables when three horsemen came up behind me at a hard gallop. I wondered what had happened that they would be in such a hurry. I soon found out! As I came up the next ridge, I saw this man. He was hanging from the branch of an oak tree and had a rope around his neck. His neck was broken!" Joseph's eyes filled with tears. He swallowed hard but continued, "What was so terrible was that his arms and legs were twitching and jerking. He looked like he was dancing a jig!"

Lynchings were not unusual in the area. Possibly the man was a horse thief, a claim jumper, or a highway robber. All such offenses warranted frontier justice and a rope around the neck. The Sextons never found out what the man was hanged for, but the memory would haunt Joseph for the rest of his life.

The continuing prosperity of the Sexton nursery was halted abruptly by a severe drought in 1864. The streams and creeks dried up. The plants, starved for water, died. It was a hard time. Richard did not waste time. He cut his losses and with the profits from his successful years in Ione, went in search of another opportunity.

The Sextons had spent ten years in Ione. Ann wished it could have been longer as it was a good life and they prospered. The rest of the country had not fared so well during this time. Ann, always an avid newspaper reader, had kept up with things. She would make a pilgrimage into town on a regular basis to collect her current copy of the *Amador County Ledger Dispatch*. For Ann, evenings were her favorite part of the day. She would sit in her rocking chair and do crocheting or needlework by the light of the lantern. But before taking up her current project, she would read the newspaper cover to cover. For some time she had been getting news from family back home that the situation over slavery and states' rights was heating up. Her extended Quaker family were staunch abolitionists, some even providing refuge on the underground railway.

It did not come as a surprise when she read in the newspaper that Fort Sumter near Charleston, South Carolina had been fired on in April 1861 and surrendered the next day to the Confederate General Beauregard. *How terribly sad,* she thought. *Surely this means war.* Ann was right. She read three months later of the First Battle of Bull Run and another Union defeat. Then Jefferson Davis became president of the Confederacy in Richmond, Virginia in November of that same year.

Ann's heart ached for her country. A year after the beginning of the war at Fort Sumter, came a report of the bloody battle at Shiloh in Tennessee. Her Quaker upbringing which focused on a pacifist stance rose in her consciousness, and she wept bitter tears. "So much waste, so much tragedy," she sobbed. In September the bloodiest of all battles took place at Antietam in Maryland. Ann shed more tears for the fallen. When conscription was initiated, many of Ann's nephews back in Ohio were called. Some were able to opt out by paying the required $300, but some had to go even though their conscience forbade them to fight. Upon learning of their beliefs, many were assigned by the military to be attendants in the hospitals.

Ann thought the war would never end. She almost gave up her commitment to read the newspaper every day, but her curiosity was too strong. She had to know what was happening to her country, even though the battles were so far away. 1863 brought the Battle of Gettysburg in Pennsylvania, then in 1864, William Tecumseh Sherman (the same man who escaped the sinking of the infamous *SS Lewis*) performed his remarkable and destructive march to Atlanta, then to the sea. The war finally ended in April 1865 when Lee surrendered to Grant at Appomattox Courthouse in Virginia.

By this time the family was settled in a new area. Ann's relief was short lived as she read the very next week that President Lincoln had been shot at Ford's Theater in Washing-ton and died the next day. Ann wept again for the great man who had led a nation in a terrible war. He accomplished a great victory and freed the slaves.

The Mother Lode was not exempt from effects of the Civil War. There were many southerners up in the hills. They tended to stick together and sometimes would gather either in their camps or in the saloons in town, singing Dixie and displaying the Confederate flag. In the bitter defeat at the end, they were even more belligerent, vowing that the south would rise again. Many brawls and killings resulted. There was no peace even in the rich hills.

$\mathscr{A}nn$

1864 - 1876

From Petaluma to Santa Barbara

THE DROUGHT AND loss of the nursery in Ione was a blow, but Richard seized this opportunity, and the forced move, to make a good investment. Just two miles west of the village of Petaluma in Sonoma County was the Stewart Nursery. It was a well established and respected business. Richard purchased considerable stock, the land, and many buildings, including a spacious house.

Although Ann dreaded the work of moving, this time she was excited about settling into her new home. It was the nicest one since leaving the farm in Hamilton County, Ohio. Her children were all with her still, but they were growing up. The three oldest boys were young men now. Elizabeth was sixteen and a real beauty. Her baby, Lewis, was almost twelve years old. Soon he would be an adolescent. Her children all treated her with much love and respect, and she considered herself blessed.

By this time, Richard was an expert horticulturalist, as were Joseph and William, who again helped with the business. The nursery was renamed the Petaluma Nursery, and the townspeople and local ranchers became loyal customers. Ann no longer had to work so hard and was even able to hire a cleaning woman to help keep up the big house. Richard, ever the astute businessman, was making even more money than up in Ione, and again, established a money lending business on the side.

The Sextons kept up their avid newspaper reading habit and early in 1867, the San Francisco paper ran an ad that caught Richard's interest: The historic La Goleta Rancho, a Mexican land grant in Santa Barbara County, had been subdivided for public sale by the heirs of the original grantee, Daniel Hill of Massachusetts, who died in 1865.

Ann knew her husband so well. As she sat beside him that evening, she could tell by the way he shifted in his chair and sat up so abruptly, that something had caught his interest. *Oh, oh, what is it this time?* she said to herself. It did not take her long to find out as Richard could never keep his excitement over a new venture to himself.

Richard showed her the ad, "I think I will go down there and see about this. It could be a good investment. While I'm there, I'll look over the soil, the climate, the availability of water and the proximity of roads going to market."

Ann sighed and gave her husband her blessing. She would miss him while he was gone, but the boys could run things efficiently. Richard's restless, entrepreneurial nature had provided well for them over the years and wasn't this the very thing she loved so in him?

Ann had to wait until his return to hear all about the trip, and she was impatient to learn what he thought. After the warm hugs of welcome, she led him to his favorite chair and pulling up one of her own sat down and faced him eagerly, "Now, please do tell me all about thy trip."

Richard leaned back with a deep sigh, "I was able to board the side wheeler Orizaba in San Francisco and in just twenty-eight hours I reached Santa Barbara. There was no wharf there, so I had to take a surf boat to shore. I assessed the area. It is truly amazing! There is a 3500-foot mountain range behind the town, and this protects the place from the winter storms from the north. There are islands, and they keep the ocean disturbances away. Most amazing of all, the shoreline runs east and west.

This means the coast faces the sun all day long. This area is ideal for agriculture and a nursery!" he exclaimed.

"Well, I take it that thou bought some of this wonderful land," Ann teased.

"But, of course. You know I would not have traveled all that way to just look at something if it was that good." Richard laughed. "First of all, I bought twelve acres in the southwestern corner of the town. It goes all the way to the beach. It will be an ideal spot for a nursery."

"That sounds good," Ann exclaimed.

"But, that is not all!" Richard exclaimed. "I took a trip eight miles west to look over that land that was advertised This was Daniel Hill's Rancho Goleta. I bought three parcels for $2,200, about one hundred acres. This area has amazing possibilities. I think we should move down there as soon as possible."

Ann agreed. She even caught Richard's excitement and appropriated it as her own.

"How could an American from Massachusetts come to own a Mexican land grant?" Ann asked.

"Now, that is an interesting story," Richard replied. "Daniel Hill had been first mate on the Boston hide and tallow ship, Rover, in 1822 when he arrived in Santa Barbara and decided to stay. He fell in love with one of the Ortega girls, Raphaela. She was a descendant of the builders of the Presidio in 1782. He converted to Catholicism and became a Mexican citizen. He married her and became eligible for a land grant which he received from Governor Pio Pico in July 1846."

"Amazing!" Ann exclaimed. "How romantic and now we own part of that history."

"Yes, we do!" Richard exclaimed.

William was left to run the Petaluma Nursery. Joseph would also stay on to help him. The rest of the family made their way by steamer to Santa Barbara. Ann took in her new home with great interest. Santa

Barbara was a sleepy adobe village of about 3,000 inhabitants, mostly Spanish-speaking.

The predominating structure was the Mission Santa Barbara, located at the mouth of Mission Canyon, two miles from the beach. Its twin towers loomed over the small settlement. Most of the structures were of adobe with tile roofs, but on the edge of town, some homes were being built of Yankee shingles and shiplap, boards with overlapping joints. Richard immediately set about building them a home at 229 Castillo Street out of redwood clapboards and dimension lumber shipped by schooner from Santa Cruz sawmills and floated ashore off West Beach. He put up a fence on the north side and planted a row of walnut trees.

Many years later, this property would become a source of legal contention. The property was originally part of what was called the Haley Survey. Captain Salisbury Haley was master of the ship, Seabird. He was contracted to survey the City of Santa Barbara for a sum of $2,000. As local folklore tells it, instead of using a surveyor's steel chain, he used a Spanish reata of braided rawhide. On foggy mornings the leather would stretch; on hot afternoons it would shrink. This resulted in a confusion of property lines, as much as thirty feet out of position.

In 1878 another survey was accepted as official by the city. Richard's fence and trees were found to go down the center of Montecito Street. The lot line had to be moved south, resulting in expenses to Richard. He initiated a lawsuit, which came to be known as the Sexton suit and was awarded $1,000.

When Joseph, up in Petaluma, heard of the beauty and potential of the land his parents had found in Santa Barbara, he headed south, leaving William to run the nursery. He built a small shack near his parent's home and started up his own nursery with 1,000 walnut seedlings. He would eventually buy the Goleta property from his father and expand his nursery to become a thriving concern. Hiring thirty Chinese workers, Joseph built a booming business in exporting pampas grass plumes which had become fashionable in adorning horses in parades. His father, Richard, was the first to import pampas grass from Argentina into California.

Ann loved Santa Barbara, with its natural beauty and delightful climate. She would often reflect on all she had experienced to get to this place. Her adventures had been remarkable, but she did not view them as such. To her, they were just necessary steps in going forth into a new land. Looking back, she could not imagine a life lived out on the farm in Ohio as she had once so desperately desired. She would not have traded the sights and scenes of her life with her Richard, for any part of that old dream.

As the years went by, one by one her children left for lives of their own. Elizabeth, now married to John Edwards, lived nearby. The Edwards brothers were neighbors up in Ione. Elizabeth and John had two children. Joseph was also married and living in Goleta. He and his wife, Lucy had four children, but if Lucy kept producing babies at the rate of one a year, there were sure to be many more. Ann doted on her grandchildren. Eventually even her baby, Lewis, traveled to Ventura County where he was raising sheep,.

Ann had fewer demands on her now, but she began to experience an increasing weariness. She found herself out of breath with the simplest exertion. *Getting old,* she thought. *It happens to everyone, and I am in my sixties now.*

One beautiful day in Santa Barbara as the sun found its way through the early morning fog, Ann walked from one room to another, idly straightening things up as she went. The now familiar breathlessness was worse than usual. As she entered the bedroom, a violent pain hit her in her chest. She gasped and clutched at herself. The pressure was incredible. She sank to the floor. The pain worsened and ran into her arms and neck with a vicious, grabbing force. Ann lay there, helpless, willing the pain to leave. Then it did seem to loosen its grip. She felt like she was floating, then the feeling left her, and she knew no more.

Ann Claypoole Sexton was buried in Santa Barbara. Her husband, Richard, and all of her children and grandchildren were there to honor this small determined woman in her plain Quaker garb. Richard recalled her loyalty and love and the courage with which she faced the dangers and difficulties of their trip west and the pioneer places they settled in. Her children remembered how she had taken care of them during the hazardous crossing of Nicaragua and on the filthy and pestilence ridden trip up to San Francisco on the Lewis. She had been a constant light in their lives. They would miss her terribly.

A portion of the thirty-first chapter of Proverbs was read at her burial:

> *"Who can know a virtuous woman,*
> *for her price is far above rubies.*
> *The heart of her husband doth safely trust in her*
> *so that he shall have no need of Spoil.*
> *She will do him good and not evil all the days of her life.*
> *Strength and honor are her clothing,*
> *and she shall rejoice in time to come.*
> *Her children arise up and call her blessed;*
> *her husband also and he praiseth her.*
> *Many daughters have done virtuously,*
> *but thou exceeded them all."*

EMMA BISBEE ON THE HONOR ROLL
AT HOLLISTER HIGH SCHOOL

EMMA AND ALMIRA (ALLIE) BISBEE

Sarah

1869 - 1880

FROM HOLLISTER TO WILMINGTON

SARAH SAT TRANSFIXED. She watched the images flashing on the white bed sheet hung at the front of the room. She had never before seen a "Magic Lantern" show and this one fascinated her. Over and over were shown scenes of the damages of strong drink. There were true-life photographs of men in taverns, poverty-stricken families victimized by a drunken breadwinner, fallen women plying their trade on the streets and people of both sexes dying in hospital wards. The pictures were terrible, but the audience was spellbound. Although there was the occasional gasp of horror, no one left the room.

The slide show was being put on by Oliver Youngblood from England. He was a member of the Band of Hope, established in 1847 in Leeds, England by a man named Jabez Tunnicliffe. In England, as well as America, hard liquor was considered a necessity of life right next to food and water. The Band of Hope had waged a campaign against the influence of pubs and brewers and held a crusade to rescue what they called "unfortunates." To accomplish this, they campaigned for complete abstinence from alcoholic beverages of any kind.

The Bisbees had moved from Ophir in 1869. The move had not pleased Sarah at first. Ophir was beautiful, and Sarah had her small house church that was the center of her life there, but Riley became restless from time to time and when some Bisbee relatives told him of the fertile soil of San Benito County south of San Francisco, the family packed up and was on its way to the town of Hollister. Now, three years later, Sarah was grateful for the move.

In 1869, the year the Bisbees came to Hollister, a Methodist Episcopal Church was established, and now there was an impressive building in town to house the growing congregation Sarah joined the church and became thoroughly involved in its activities. She was now teaching a Sunday school class, was a member of the women's society, the missionary society, and attended a weekly Bible study. The church was her inspiration and solace from an unhappy marriage.

This presentation by the Band of Hope representative was held in the church's social hall and was well attended. At the end of the lecture Mr. Youngblood asked for all in the audience to voluntarily sign a pledge never to drink alcoholic beverages. He passed out small white cards and pencils.

It was not a hard decision for Sarah to make. She had only tasted wine once and hated it, at that time making a decision to leave it alone forever. She thought back to all the examples of destructive drunkenness she had seen. She remembered the problems of the canal workers back in Indiana, who drank up their wages and left their families to go hungry. Scenes from the ships that had taken her to Panama and California jumped into her mind; the drunken gatherings of men in the cabins and staggering up on deck. She could see the slatternly Dolly O'Neal and smell her foul breath as she staggered toward Sarah to offer her a "job." Even in lovely Ophir, tavern brawls occurred on a regular basis, and then there was the problem at home. Riley still drank to excess from time to time, and although he worked hard and provided for his family, his volatile moods were grievous to her.

She eagerly signed the pledge card and vowed to herself to do what she could in the future to help with this campaign.

Hollister was situated in a fertile, broad valley. It was a prosperous town due to the success of the local farming enterprises. There were abundant orchards of fruit trees, mostly apricots, pears and peaches. Ironically, vineyards supplying grapes for local wineries dotted the landscape. Many fields of potatoes and cabbages covered the valley. The climate, along with the fertile black soil, created an ideal agrarian locale.

Nearby was the Mission San Juan Bautista, founded in 1797. The Spanish style adobe structure was surrounded by barracks, originally built to house soldiers, a nunnery, and the Jose Castro house. These were arranged around a grassy plaza. In its day, the mission ministered to the local Ohlone Indians and later to the Yokuts from the Central Valley.

In Sarah's time, a small town had grown up around the mission, inhabited mostly by Spanish speaking Catholics. The mission had fallen into some disrepair, but it would be lovingly restored shortly after Sarah and her family moved on. Sarah had mixed feelings when she visited the mission. Her suspicion of anything Catholic tainted her view. Yes, it was picturesque and charming, and perhaps those friars helped the Indians, but just maybe they exploited them too.

Another advantage of Hollister was the school system. It was possible for Sarah's children to receive a good education here and she rejoiced in this. She had never recovered from the blow of her aborted schooling. Perhaps due to her reverence for education, the children did exceptionally well in school, often making the honor roll for both studies and deportment. She was proud of them. She also saw that they attended church and Sunday school on a regular basis. During the morning worship service, their mother allowed no fidgeting, and she would often quiz them on the sermon's content on the way home. Sarah was determined to raise her children to be staunch Methodists.

Riley found the Hollister area to his liking in its productivity and progressiveness. There were longer periods of peace in the home, but sometimes out of nowhere, he would sink into one of his black moods and again he would be irritable and impossible to please. Sarah continued to walk a precarious line in their relationship. She was particularly concerned about the children, wanting to protect them from the outpouring of their father's wrath. Sometimes that proved to be an impossible task and family discord prevailed for a time, until Riley would emerge on the other side in a calmer state.

Marital relations between Sarah and Riley had all but ceased. They still slept in the same bed, but often retired at different times. One would be sound asleep when the other came to bed. Sarah remembered the eager coming together of the years up on the Sacramento before that river went into its rampage and destroyed their life there. It had never been the same since between them. Sarah accepted this as the way it was, so one night when Riley reached for her, she was surprised but did not resist. That one night would result in the advent of yet another child, much to Sarah's surprise.

It had been five years since the birth of Frederick, and she thought she was through with childbearing. Both the pregnancy and delivery were difficult. It seemed her body had forgotten how to nurture and bring forth babies. Yet, on January 10, 1872, after a long labor, Sarah delivered another baby boy, Walter Riley Bisbee. She gave him his middle name after his father because she still had a deep fondness for her husband, in spite of their difficulties. Baby Walter was healthy and a good baby. In spite of her misgivings about another child, Sarah doted on the baby.

The Hollister ME Church organized a chapter of the Band of Hope and Sarah joined right away, becoming a charter member of the group. She educated herself on the battle against alcohol and the next year she became the secretary. She was convinced she was at least a small part of the solution to a pressing social problem.

As the year 1876 rolled around Sarah began to sense a familiar restlessness in Riley. *I think another move is in the offing,* she told herself. Sure enough, several months later he expressed his interest in moving farther south, this time to Los Angeles County. As usual, he had heard from a relative that the farming was extremely promising there. It seemed that the Bisbees had relatives in every part of California. Riley made a trip south to look the situation over and shortly after that, the family found itself on the way to the town of Wilmington, near the City of Angels.

Sarah felt thankful for two very important things: All of her children were still at home and there was an abundance of Methodist churches in southern California. There was a very active one near their new home.

Sarah was at the door of the church the first Sunday after their arrival. She soon wrote for her letter of transfer of membership as well as that of her children. It was a proud day for her when the whole family, minus Riley, walked to the front of the church to be received into membership. The pastor, on his part, was gratified to find such an ardent church worker in his new adult member. She was put to work right away teaching a Sunday school class.

At first, disappointed that there was not a chapter of the Band of Hope in her new church home, she discovered something even more exciting. The movement against alcohol had grown, and a new organization had sprung up in Evanston, Illinois in 1873. It spread eastward to New York, where women mobilized and entered the local saloons, singing, praying, and urging the owners to stop selling alcohol. This group was the first to adopt a new name, The Woman's Christian Temperance Union. It became a national organization a year later in Cleveland, Ohio.

Annie Wittenmyer became the first president of the WCTU. She was a woman intently focused on the alcohol problem. The second president, a woman called Frances Willard, greatly expanded the work and vision of the organization. Under her leadership, they branched out in a reform agenda, now embracing women's rights, education and the re-form of prostitutes and prisoners. Frances Willard was a strong advocate of women's suffrage, feeling that the vote of women would purify the nation. Under Willard's leadership, the WCTU moved westward as a strong force. Sarah's church adopted this organization with enthusiasm and one of the most enthusiastic was Sarah Bisbee.

By 1880, Sarah, at forty-four, was living a satisfying life, with her children, her church work and her involvement in the WCTU. Only her marriage lacked any vitality and Sarah paid less attention to that problem than ever before because she was so busy. Chauncey was twenty-four now, a man grown. He worked with his father on the farm. Allie, twenty-two, had finished her training as a teacher and had a second-grade class in the local elementary school. Emma, twenty, and Ada, eighteen were each completing their teacher training. Sarah was so proud of her girls, fulfilling her old ambition to become a teacher herself. Frederick, fourteen, and Walter, eight, were in school nearby.

With the children all at home and involved in their own activities, she was able to give even more time to the work of the WCTU. She was elected to various offices, from secretary to vice president, then for several years as president. Sarah worked hard on her own to perfect her writing skills and her use of the English language. It stood her in good stead in her new roles. She found herself the speaker on many occasion, starting with the local group and expanding to regional meetings. She also began to get involved in the suffrage movement, feeling strongly that women needed an equal voice. It was exhilarating. Her speaking ability improved with use and she found herself in demand.

One day in 1880, Chauncey, happened to mention that a new family had purchased a farm in nearby Compton. The purchaser was a Lewis Sexton and his wife, Ella.

Sarah half listened to the report when something struck her. "That name, Sexton, is familiar," she commented. "I once met a lady in San Francisco, a long time ago with that same last name. I wonder if there is any connection."

The Next Generation

EMMA BISBEE

LEWIS SEXTON

MAY AUGUSTA SEXTON, AGE 3

Emma

1885

An Unusual Love Story

EMMA MINNETTA BISBEE was in love. Madly, passionately in love.

This was a state Emma never thought to find herself in. Intelligent, determined, self-sufficient, she had her life planned out. One thing she had not planned on, however, was a person in her life who had the ability to turn everything upside down. Now, at twenty-six, she could see that her plans might have to change.

As Emma guided her horse and buggy down the road to the home of her beloved, she thought back over her life so far. Yet, her confused memory of the terrible flood of the Sacramento, Feather, and Yuba rivers was all she could pull up. She remembered being awakened by her Mama Sarah who thrust her clothing over her head. There was a flash of the wagon with a tarpaulin overhead and rain...lots and lots of rain. She had been frightened and confused. The anxious voices and shouting of other refugees rang in her memory.

The time she spent in Sacramento was also a blur. But she remembered being glad to have her cousin, Mary Theresa, to play with, as well as her brother, Chauncey, and sister, Allie. Her sister, Ada, was just a tiny baby then, but Emma loved holding her. A bond began there between them that continued to this day.

Emma loved living in Ophir. Life settled down there to a routine. She started school in this lovely valley. From the first day, she was thrilled with learning new things. Mama Sarah had always stressed the importance of education to her children, and in Emma, she found an eager disciple. Emma journeyed to the little house church with her mother, brother, and sisters on a regular basis. She learned to sit still and not fidget even if she did not completely understand what was going on. For a time Mama Sarah taught her Sunday school class. She loved her time there.

Emma did not want to move to Hollister, but at ten-years-old, she soon realized that the educational opportunities for her were much better there than in Ophir. She continued to love school and excelled both academically and in deportment. She was so proud when her name appeared on the school honor roll in the local paper.

Emma's older sister, Allie, became a teacher. Emma and Ada vowed to follow in her footsteps. This goal inevitably came from Mama Sarah's thwarted dream of becoming a teacher herself. Now, all three daughters were actively pursuing this calling.

Emma wondered what might have happened if the family had not moved to Wilmington in Los Angeles County. She was able to finish her teacher training at the impressive new California State Normal School, and she absolutely loved her class of eighth-graders presently under her tutelage. Allie married and gave up teaching to have a family, but Emma and Ada were still following their profession of choice. The two were very close and talked together often about their futures. They vowed to stay single and continue their careers.

"I do not care at all if everyone calls us old maid school teachers. That is what I want to do," Emma stated emphatically.

Ada was somewhat less adamant about the career choice. "I don't know, Emma. I certainly plan to stay unmarried, but I have been thinking about changing from teaching to working for the church. I feel God leading me in this direction." Both young women were committed in their loyalty to their church, but Emma had definitely not felt the calling Ada had. However, she respected Ada's choice.

The motivation to stay single was not hard to decipher. Their parents' marriage was anything but happy. The young women adored their mother, Sarah. Her courage and intelligence were awe inspiring. They loved their father, Riley, but at times he was difficult and unpredictable. The pain in Sarah's face at these times did not escape their notice. Emma realized that she would not have existed at all but for her parents' union and she would love to have children, but her students were an excellent substitute. The future seemed clear.

She thought back to the day three years ago when she went with her mother to call on the new neighbors. As they sat side by side in the buggy, Emma thought that no one would recognize them as mother and daughter. Emma was not pretty in the traditional sense but could be described as "handsome' with her abundant dark hair and brows set in a narrow face. She thought that perhaps she was a throwback to some Irish ancestor. Sarah now had iron grey hair pulled severely into a bun and her finely wrinkled face attested to the hard life she had experienced. Only in their straight and determined backs were they identical.

Emma did not know it then, but this visit would change the course of her life. Sarah was in an excited mood as they made their way to Compton. "I met a woman of this name a long time ago in San Francisco," Sarah stated as she guided the horse in the direction of the new Sexton ranch. "I just wonder if there is a connection."

A handsome, stately lady met them at the door. Sarah spoke first. "I am Mrs. Riley Bisbee, your neighbor, and this is my daughter, Emma. We came to welcome you to the neighborhood."

The lady smiled, her face lighting up. "I am Ella Sexton. I am so glad to meet you. Please do come in."

They were led into a small parlor. Sarah and Emma seated

themselves on a velvet settee as Ella excused herself to go make the tea. She soon returned with a tray containing a china pot of tea, three matching cups and saucers of what appeared to be English bone china and a plate of cookies. Ella told them that she and her husband, Lewis Sexton, had moved from Ventura where her husband had been raising sheep. He had bought this farmland and planned to grow crops here as well as sell wood from the large grove of eucalyptus trees. Ella explained that they had married in Ventura.

As their pleasant conversation continued, a back door slammed, and soon a tall, dark-haired man came into the parlor. He was handsome, with an erect carriage and a neatly trimmed beard. "How wonderful that you happened to come home, dear. Now you can meet our neighbors, the Bisbees," Ella exclaimed. Turning to Sarah and Emma, she said, "This is my husband, Lewis."

Lewis bowed rather elegantly to the two and said, "I am pleased to meet you. You are so kind to come calling."

Sarah could not help herself, she had to ask. "You know, many, many years ago when I was just a girl of eighteen, I met a woman in San Francisco by the name of Ann Sexton. Could you possibly be related?"

A look of surprise swept over Lewis' face. "That would be my mother. Her name was Ann Sexton."

Sarah's heart started pounding. She had never forgotten her time with this lady and here was one of her sons living almost next door. "I was working in a tailor shop. Your mother came in with three of her sons. She wanted some trousers made for them. She wanted them to last. That is why she did not buy them at a dry goods store. Were you one of those boys?

"No, I wasn't there. I was the baby, but I remember those pants. They were handed down to me in good time. They were so well made, they lasted that long."

"This is wonderful! What a coincidence. And how is your mother?

She was such a lovely lady?"

"I am sorry to tell you that she passed away several years ago from a heart attack. She is buried in Santa Barbara where the family finally settled."

"I am so sorry," Sarah exclaimed. "You know, I made her tea, and we had a good conversation when she came to pick up the pants. We had both crossed Central America almost at the same time, actually three months apart. Your family came across Nicaragua, and I came across Panama. We compared the difficulties, and we both had awful experiences on the ships to San Francisco."

"I was too young to remember any of that, but I memorized the stories my parents and brothers and sister told, so it almost seemed that I remembered it." Lewis sighed.

"I knew we would not meet again," Sarah replied. "We were both about to leave San Francisco for other places, but I was so impressed with your mother and her courage, taking care of five children in those conditions."

"Yes," Lewis stated. "My mother was an incredible woman."

As Sarah and Emma drove home, they commented on their visit. "I think the Sextons are about to add to their family," Sarah observed.

"That's nice," Emma replied absently. Suddenly, she focused, "I can't believe you met his mother in San Francisco and that they crossed over Central America at about the same time. Life is strange, isn't it?" At that time, Emma had no idea just how strange it could be.

A few months later, word reached the Bisbee household that the Sextons had a new baby girl named May Augusta. They sent a handmade baby gift for the new arrival. A few months after that they were shocked and saddened to hear that Ella Sexton had died. She never recovered from the difficult birth of her baby. The Bisbees sent their condolences.

Emma shook herself slightly. Enough daydreaming, she thought.

I am almost there. She could hardly contain her excitement. Tying the horse's reins to the hitching post, Emma alighted from the buggy and knocked on the door. Her breath came in gasps. She was about to again be with the person she loved.

Lewis opened the door and smiled. Behind him, a squeal split the air, "Auntie Emma! Auntie Emma! You're here!"

Chubby legs propelled the small child across the room. Blue eyes flashing, blond curls bouncing, May Augusta leapt into Emma's arms.

Hugging her tightly, Emma murmured, "Yes, Baby May, I am here, and I am going to take you for an afternoon adventure." Emma was as ecstatic as the three-year-old. What better than to spend some hours with the love of her life.

As they started to leave, Lewis spoke softly, "When you bring May back, I would like to talk to you about something." He hesitated, then continued, "It's important."

Emma slowed her step. She knew that this moment might present itself. She had debated the outcome in her mind many times. Now it was upon her. "Yes, I think we do have something important to talk about. I shall see you when I bring May home."

THE SEXTON FAMILY 1892

GRACE 6, GLEN 4, EMMA 33, MAY 10, EARL 6 MO.

SISTERS TOGETHER – GRACE AND MAY

THE SEXTON FAMILY 1904
GLEN, GRACE, EMMA, EARL

$\mathcal{E}mma$

1885-1893

COMING TOGETHER AND LETTING GO

EMMA FELT A twinge of anxiety as she returned to the Sexton ranch with a tired May by her side on the buggy seat. Her meeting with Lewis could hold her future in its outcome. Lewis must have seen them coming. He opened the door and reached for his daughter.

May, who although drooping in the buggy suddenly revived and started chattering. "Oh Papa, we had such a good time! Auntie Emma and me, we cut out paper dolls, and we baked cookies, and we worked on our scrapbook, and Auntie Emma taught me a new song."

She finally ran out of breath. Slipping down, May ran to her small chair in the parlor and holding a small package started to pull out paper dolls and cookies helter-skelter.

"Whoa, Baby May," Emma remonstrated. "Slow down a bit. The cookies are for after your supper. Papa will give them to you if you eat everything you should."

By now, Lewis was laughing heartily at his irrepressible daughter. "I have her supper ready," he said.

Emma offered, "Why don't I feed her and put her to bed. She is surely exhausted."

"Yes, I would like that," Lewis responded. "Then we can have our talk."

Emma fed May a small bowl of soup and some bread and butter. After finishing this, she ate two cookies. Emma could see her bright eyes getting heavy. She picked the child up and carried her upstairs to her room where she helped her get into her nightgown.

When May was nestled in her little bed, she begged. "Tell me a story, Auntie Emma."

"Just a short one, Baby May." As Emma started on May's favorite story, she did not progress far until she saw May was fast asleep. Tucking the soft quilt around her, Emma faced what was to come and made her way downstairs. Lewis was waiting for her in the parlor. Emma sat on a chair facing him and waited.

"Miss Bisbee, you have been a godsend for my daughter. The time you spend with her is invaluable. She has come to love you."

"And I love her with all my heart," Emma responded.

Lewis cleared his throat and continued, "I was wondering if you would consider marrying me and becoming a mother to May. I admire you very much Miss Bisbee, and I think you would make a fine wife and mother."

This was exactly what Emma had been expecting. She had thought about the possibility as she lay awake far into the night. Lewis Sexton was a fine looking man and an honorable one from a good family. She also admired him a great deal, but marriage had never been in her life plan. Now here it was being offered to her. If there had been no three-year-old angel child, Emma would have refused and kept on her well-charted life course, but here was a chance to become May's mother and she could not pass this by.

"I consider it an honor to marry you and to be May's mother.

Would you please now call me Emma?"

Lewis smiled with apparent happiness, "I am so glad. And you may call me Lewis."

Emma sighed, then she smiled back. With her usual forthrightness, she exclaimed, "I do believe you will make an excellent husband, Lewis!"

Lewis burst out laughing. "I plan to do just that. Now, when shall we set the date?" After a short discussion, they agreed on a date two months away.

As Emma left to go home, Lewis took her hands in his and reaching forward kissed her on the cheek. "You have made me very happy. May will be overjoyed. She never knew her mother. She truly needs one."

Emma Bisbee and Lewis Sexton were married in the Methodist Episcopal Church with just their families in attendance. Ada was Emma's maid of honor, and May was the flower girl. After a simple reception, May came up to Emma. "Can I ask you something?" she lisped.

"What is it, little one?" Emma queried as she stooped down to hear her better.

"Auntie Emma, can I call you Mama Emma now?"

"Oh, yes, yes, yes! You may certainly call me that because now I am your mama."

May skipped off murmuring, "Mama Emma, Mama Emma."

Emma moved into the big house on the Sexton ranch. She had resigned from her teaching position at the end of the school year and now dedicated herself fully to being a ranch wife and mother. Sarah had taught her daughter well. She was a good manager and an even better cook. The new routine suited her. Lewis was a kind and gentle husband and spending whole days with her love of a daughter was Emma's idea of heaven.

A few months after the wedding, Emma realized that she might be going to have a little sister or brother for May. It was something of a surprise, but as she became more sure of the reality of this, she found herself extremely happy. Pregnancy could still be a dangerous journey for a woman in the 1880's, but Emma was strong and healthy and did not anticipate any difficulties. On September 25, 1886, a baby daughter, Grace Ellen, was born to Lewis and Emma. May was beside herself with excitement over the arrival of a baby sister. Now four, she prided herself on being Mama Emma's helper. She was determined that she would help take care of this new arrival.

As expected, May became a little mother to baby Grace. By the time the toddler was walking and into everything, May was her constant companion. Just a little over two years after the arrival of Grace, the Sextons welcomed a baby boy, Lewis Glen, into their home. The farming was going well. Lewis had absorbed the horticultural interests of his family and did well in agriculture. He raised bumper crops of alfalfa and barley. The sale of wood from the gum or eucalyptus trees brought in a substantial income. Emma was pleased when they were chosen for an article in a volume of *The History of Los Angeles County*. She knew that Lewis was pleased, as his brother, William, had achieved a similar write up in *The History of Ventura County* and his brother, Joseph with his burgeoning citrus and pampas grass industry in Santa Barbara was one of that town's leading citizens.

Four years after the arrival of little Lewis Glen, Emma gave birth to another son, Carl Earl. Now with two lovely girls and two robust boys, Emma felt her life to be complete. As she was soon to learn, it is dangerous to become too smug about your good fortune.

One sunny June afternoon, Lewis came in from the fields and sank into a kitchen chair. Emma turned from the stove where she was frying a chicken for their supper. "What's wrong, Lewis, you look so pale."

"I don't know, Emma dear, I am feeling very strange. I have no energy, and I ache all over."

Emma rushed to Lewis's side and put her hand on his forehead, then the back of his neck. "You're burning up with fever. Come upstairs, I'll help you to bed." Emma pushed the pan of chicken to the back of the stove and taking Lewis's handled him up the stairs.

Emma called to ten-year-old May to take over the supper preparation and feed her brother and sister. Baby Earl at six months was still nursing. She helped Lewis undress and get into bed, pulling the covers up over him. Running back downstairs, she pumped some cool water into a basin and returning to the bedside, sponged her husband's face and body. Emma did not sleep much that night, alternately sponging his fevered body and pulling more covers over him when he shook with chills. At times he became delirious.

The next morning when a neighbor stopped by, Emma asked him to go for the doctor. It was several hours before he arrived, but after examining Lewis, the doctor turned to Emma, "He has influenza and a bad case at that. I'm afraid all you can do is try to get the fever down as you have been and let it run its course. I will come by tomorrow to check on him."

May practically took over the household chores and taking care of Grace and Glen. Emma only took time to nurse, bathe and dress baby Earl. Otherwise, she was at Lewis's bedside, repeatedly sponging him off and comforting him.

On the third day of his illness, she thought he might be getting better as his eyes cleared and he looked at her to say, "You have been such a good wife, Emma, and a wonderful mother. I do love you."

"I love you too," she said softly. "Now, just get better. I need you."

Not long after this exchange, she noticed that his breathing seemed to become more difficult. Soon he was gasping for breath. Emma tried to get him into a sitting position to ease his airways, but it did not help. His struggle continued for a while, then suddenly he relaxed in her arms. Emma laid Lewis back on the pillow and desperately felt for a pulse, but there was none. Her husband of eight years was gone. She laid her head on his chest and let out a choked cry. Then Emma gathered her inner resources and sat up. She had four small children to care for. There would be time for grieving later.

Emma and Sarah

1893

MORE ILLNESS AND A LEAVING

LEWIS SEXTON WAS buried at Rosedale Cemetery in Los Angeles. Emma stood by the open grave as his casket was lowered. She clutched baby Earl to her breast as her other three children clung to her in a grieving cluster of confusion. Her heart ached, but the tears did not come. Emma and the children rode back to her house in her parents' wagon.

Once there, Sarah sent Riley on home. "This family needs looking after right now. I'll just stay until things settle down," Sarah told her husband.

Sarah cooked chicken soup for their supper. Chicken soup always seemed to soothe those partaking of it Sarah thought. The children ate, but Sarah noticed that Emma hardly touched her food. "Mama," she sighed, "I am exhausted. I hurt all over. I think I will go straight to bed. Will you see that the children are looked after?"

Sarah gave her daughter a worried look. "Of course I will. Is there anything I can get you?"

"No," Emma replied, "I just need some sleep. I've barely slept for days."

Later, after the children were in bed and asleep, Sarah peeked into

Emma's room. She thought that Emma's breathing was more labored than usual. She tiptoed over to the bed and laid her hand gently on her daughter's forehead. It was very hot. Sarah came to the conclusion that Emma now had come down with influenza, undoubtedly contracted from her husband, Lewis. Sarah's heart sank. She had been very fond of Lewis, and his loss had affected her deeply. Was she now to lose her beloved daughter too?

At that moment, death seemed to press down on her. She had lost her next to youngest son, Frederick, three years before in an accident at his work site up in Watsonville. She was still grieving for him. Then Lewis. Now the possibility of losing Emma loomed. Would her grandchildren all become sick and die too?

Emma was nursing Earl, how could he avoid coming down with this terrible disease. Sarah thought back to her journey to California across Panama and on the filthy ship to San Francisco. There was disease and death all around her then, and yet she remained well through it all, even when severely malnourished. She had amazing physical and emotional strength in her that had served her well. She just prayed to her Lord that her daughter had inherited it.

Sarah sat by Emma's bedside all night and bathed her forehead. She cooked the children porridge when they woke up the next morning. She was in a dilemma as to what to do with the baby. She made a decision. She fashioned a nursing bottle out of a narrow jar and a clean rag. She boiled and cooled some milk and sweetened it with a little molasses. Protesting at first, the baby soon sucked eagerly. Later she helped Emma express the milk from her swollen breasts and promptly threw it away. The children and especially the baby had already been exposed to the illness, but Sarah vowed to do the best she could to isolate Emma until she got through this.

The days seemed to run together for Sarah. Between the time she spent trying to bring Emma's fever down and feeding and caring for the children, she approached a state of exhaustion. Relying on her inherent strength and resistance to illness to take her through, she kept going, snatching small segments of sleep when she could. May was a great help to her, but she tried not to burden her too much as she was only a girl of ten.

Several days later, Emma's fever broke. She opened her eyes and looking at Sarah, smiled a weak smile. "Mama, I think the worst is over!" she whispered.

Sarah reached for the basin of water and started to sponge Emma's sweaty body. That evening, with clean linen on the bed, Emma was able to sit up and sip a bowl of broth. Sarah gave thanks that her Lord had brought her loved one through. Each day Emma gained strength and was finally able to get up and around for several hours during the day. Sarah rejoiced in this, but was still wary. Only until enough days had passed without any of the children getting sick could she heave a huge sigh of relief. Things were returning to normal, at least as normal as they could be with the recent loss of a beloved husband and father.

As Emma's strength returned, she became restless. There was so much to do. She now had a hundred-and-forty acre farm to run. The alfalfa and barley would soon need harvesting. She needed to locate and hire crews and equipment for the harvest. She also needed to start making plans to cut and sell the blue-gum wood. It was now up to her to support her four young children and herself. She could not waste any time. She needed to get organized.

Sarah saw her daughter's agitation and made a decision to stay on to help out. The baby, of course, required constant attention. Emma was nursing him again, but she could not spare much time to hold or rock him. The older children were out of school for the summer, but they needed to be fed and supervised. May was a regular little mother to Earl and could do some of the cooking. At seven, Grace tried to keep up with her adored older sister by being helpful. Glen was only five, and while a good child, needed to be watched. His older sisters helped with that chore.

Sarah sent word to Riley that she would be staying on for a while to help out. He did not respond. Emma organized the harvest, and it went well. Once cut, no rain came to spoil the crops as they lay in the field. She was able to sell both the alfalfa and barley at a good price, keeping only enough for the small number of livestock.

The production and sale of blue-gum wood or eucalyptus had become a growing business in Southern California. Eucalyptus had been imported from Australia where it was a native plant. It had thrived in the warm, dry, California climate. The residents still heated with wood, especially in Southern California where the winters could be both wet and cold. There were few native trees to supply wood as most had been destroyed as the population grew. Eucalyptus grew extremely rapidly. Trees that Lewis planted when first moving to the Compton farm grew so fast that in just a few years they were almost a foot across and forty to sixty feet high.

Emma went to the bank in town and borrowed enough money to harvest the trees. She knew she would be able to sell the wood at a good price and repay the loan in a timely manner. She hired a crew of Mexicans to cut and stack the wood, paying two dollars and fifty cents a cord. She sold the wood for five dollars a cord. She had picked up enough Spanish to communicate her orders to the crew, and she was a tough boss. She allowed no slacking off, but she was fair, and the wage was good for the times. They came to respect her. In the coming years, most of this crew would work for her as more trees were planted and harvested.

The summer slipped away. The children would be returning to school in a few days. The bulk of the harvest was over. Sarah had not been home except for short trips to fetch something she needed and to take Riley a pot of soup or stew and homemade bread to supplement his bachelor cooking. All of their children were out on their own now. Even

Ada had moved out and had her own place. Ada, in particular, and a few of her siblings came by to see their mother and to check on their father from time to time. Sarah needed to make a decision. In some ways, it was easy, in others, very difficult.

One evening as dusk fell, she lit the kerosene lamp and sat down at the kitchen table. She had made a pot of tea and asked Emma to join her.

"I have something I want to discuss with you," Sarah spoke directly to her daughter. Emma seated herself, and Sarah poured her a cup of tea. "What would you think of me staying with you and the children permanently?"

Emma sighed and looked into her mother's eyes. "I would love that, Mama. You are my rock, and I have come to depend on your help, but…"

"I know, I know," Sarah interrupted, "What about your papa? I have thought long and hard about this, believe me. I still care about him, but he is just impossible to live with. You cannot know how I have treasured this time here with you. We both work hard, and we respect each other. We have had a few cross words with each other when we're tired, but that is nothing. It has been hard to put up with the meanness and the rages from your father. I have not complained to you or any of your brothers or sisters, but it has been difficult. If you still need me here, I would cherish the thought of living here permanently."

Emma took her mother's hands in her own and looking into her eyes said, "Mama, it is your decision. I would love to have you here forever, and the children would welcome you too. Whichever way you decide, I will support you."

"Thank you so much. I have already thought this through. I made a decision that if you wanted me here, I would come on a permanent basis. Tomorrow I will take your horse and buggy with your permission and go tell your father of my plans. I will pack up the rest of my things and bring them here. This will not be an easy thing to do, but I believe it is the right thing. It is time I set my foot down and put an end to his bad treatment of me."

The next morning, Sarah set out. This time she did not take any food with her. *I have to end this, I need to make a clean break.*

As she approached her home in nearby Wilmington, her heart was pounding. She was a devout Christian woman, and she was making a decision that might be frowned on by her fellow churchgoers, but she knew it was time to end something that had caused her so much pain for years.

It was a chilly day in early fall, but Sarah was unaware of her surroundings, her eyes and mind focused on the house as she approached. Smoke was coming from the chimney. She hoped she was early enough to catch Riley before he left for the fields. She tied up the horse and pushed open the door. She did not knock. This was still her home even though she was leaving it today for good.

Riley was sitting at the kitchen table drinking a cup of coffee. He looked up, surprised. "Sarah! I wasn't expecting you today." Noticing her empty hands, he commented, "What, no food for a hungry bachelor? Or does this mean you're coming home? Surely Emma can manage by herself now."

Sarah looked around the kitchen. Dirty dishes and encrusted pots and pans littered the table and the sink. The stove needed blacking and the floor stuck to her shoes. Riley was a terrible housekeeper. A wave of guilt swept over her. She had to hold herself back from pitching in to fix this mess. It took all her strength just to ignore it and pull up a chair and sit down.

"Riley, I need to talk to you," Sarah started, and Riley immediately began to interrupt her. "Stop! Please be quiet and just listen. I have come to get the rest of my things. I am going to stay at Emma's for good. I am leaving you, Riley."

He opened his mouth to protest, but Sarah was adamant, "Let me finish! Your temper and your moods have made my life miserable for years. I deserve a life of peace and harmony. I believe I have found that at Emma's, and yes, she and the children do need me. Just running the farm is a full-time job for her."

"Are you finished?" Riley snorted sarcastically.

"Yes, but do not, I say, do not try to change my mind. It is too late for that."

"All right, Sarah, if this is what you want. I know I have not been easy to live with. If you change your mind, and I think you will, you can come back."

Sarah stood up and pushed her chair under the table. "I will not be coming back, Riley…ever!"

They did not say another word to each other as Sarah packed up her things. She took her clothes, her good china and some good linens, but left the everyday dishes and pots and pans as well as all of the furniture for Riley. She loaded the boxes and bags into the carriage by herself. Riley ignored her.

As she opened the kitchen door to make her final departure, she turned, "Goodbye Riley. I know Ada will be by to help you on a regular basis and Chauncey and Allie will come by also. Take care."

She walked out and climbed up in the buggy. As she drove toward her new home, she thought, *Emma and I are two strong women, and now we have to get along without men in our lives, but we will be all right. Yes, we will be just fine!*

Family Reunion 1898. Back row: Emma Bisbee Sexton 39,
May Sexton 16, Matthew Reasoner 23

Middle row: Katie Malone Reasoner 61, Earl Sexton 4,
Sarah Malone Bisbee 66

Bottom row: Grace Sexton 10, Glen Sexton 8

Katherine (Katie) Reasoner
And her son, Matthew

Emma

1893 - 1903

A Fire and More Loss

THINGS SETTLED DOWN, and life in Emma's household found a comfortable rhythm. Sarah was an invaluable help with the children and household tasks. Emma found her niche in the management of the farm. Crops were planted and harvested. Wood was sold and trees planted. Emma branched out into a new enterprise. Some farmers in nearby Watts had started truck gardens to supply the city of Los Angeles. Emma thought about doing the same, but after researching the demand, she decided to specialize in supplying vegetables like Napa cabbage, bok choy, and daikon radishes to groceries and restaurants in the flourishing China Town district of Los Angeles. She soon built up a clientele of faithful customers. The children loved to see the Chinese men arrive in their carts. In their embroidered tunics and pantaloons, with long pigtails hanging down their backs, they were exotic visitors to the Sexton ranch.

Emma insisted that Sarah continue her involvement in her organizations that she loved. Still active in the Woman's Christian Temperance Union, Sarah now was on the state board. When Frances Willard came to Los Angeles to speak, Sarah was on the welcoming committee. She also stayed in touch with the suffrage movement and occasionally marched in their parades. Both Sarah and Emma were elated when the state legislature finally approved the vote for California women in 1893. However, their joy was short lived as the governor vetoed the bill as unconstitutional.

Three years later in 1896, a state referendum defeated women's suffrage. Sarah and her fellow suffragists were not going to let the referendum sway them and were determined to fight even harder.

One cloudy winter afternoon in early 1900, the children came home from school as usual. Sarah sent them upstairs to change into their play clothes. She was putting out a plate of cookies for a snack when May and Grace flew down the stairs followed by the boys. They were in a state of dishevelment, obviously in a panic. Frightened voices started shouting. "Fire! Fire! There's fire upstairs. It's coming down the hall!"

Looking up the stairs, Sarah could see smoke and flames licking at the banister. Gathering the children, she pushed and shoved them out the door. "Out, out, out!!" she cried.

Sarah drew a deep breath. She deliberately slowed down her breathing and her heart rate. *This is bad!* she thought. *I need to get out too, but do I have time to take anything with me?*

She moved quickly to the roll-top desk in the corner of the dining room. The desk had belonged to Lewis, and Emma had taken it over and used it to organize her business with the farm. Sarah picked up the bag of laundry that sat by the door waiting for wash day. She emptied out the soiled clothes, then ran to the desk and dumped all of the miscellaneous papers into it. She noted with relief that most of the family photos were there also. Completing this chore, she ran out the kitchen door to join the terrified children.

"Oh, Grandma," Glen cried, "I thought the fire had got you!"

"Not a chance," Sarah breathed, "I just had to get some important things first."

Emma had seen the smoke from the field where she was supervising her work crew. She came riding up with the wagon and together the family watched the fiery destruction of their home. One of their neighbors had a telephone and notified the Wilmington Fire Department, but by the time they drove up, their horses at a gallop, the house was engulfed in flames.

The shocked family sat on a grassy knoll and stared at the remains of their home. The younger children started to cry. Emma saw that May let tears slide down her face. Sarah sat silent. Of all her remarkable life experiences, including two terrible floods, she never lived through a fire. So now she had.

Emma, marshaling her practical strength, said, "The important thing is that you all got out. We are all here, and we are well, and we will get through this."

Emma made the decision to take the family to Chauncey's place in Los Angeles. They climbed into the wagon and set out. Chauncey, his second wife, five-month-old daughter and two stepchildren lived near the University of Southern California. Emma's family had visited them often, so they found their way there easily. The Chauncey Bisbee family was surprised to see the bedraggled passengers in their wagon. The children were barely dressed. Emma and Sarah were in their workaday clothing and had a shocked, weary look on their faces.

"What happened?" Chauncey asked as he tied up the horses.

"Fire! It was a fire. Our house is gone!" Emma stated.

"You poor things. Come in, come in. We'll take care of you, don't you worry."

The family climbed down from the wagon. Once inside, they collapsed onto chairs. Chauncey's wife hurried to make them tea.

"I think it was a flue fire. It could have started in the attic. It was burning in the upstairs hall when the children went up to change their clothes after they came home from school," Sarah spoke up, "Whatever caused it, the house is completely gone."

Sarah and Emma's church heard about the family's plight and put on a clothing drive, bringing over boxes of children's and adult women's clothes. That, with hand me downs from Chauncey's two stepchildren, helped to outfit the four Sexton children.

Emma made several trips that week out to the farm to see to the wood cutting. She allowed the children to stay home, but the following week she told them to get dressed for school. She packed their lunches and herded them out the door and into the wagon. After dropping them off she would work out on the farm.

She dreaded the task, but one day she decided to visit the remains of her home and poke through the ashes to see if she could find anything worth salvaging. She found a few teaspoons and a jar full of coins, but little else. *Thank you, Lord, for my mother and her quick thinking. All I need for running the farm I still have,* she prayed to herself.

Emma knew her family could not stay with Chauncey forever, so she began to think of her alternatives. She could rebuild on the farm, but for some reason she did not feel this was the right thing to do, especially since had been contemplating selling some of the land and moving anyway.

She had seen a comfortable house for sale near Chauncey's that she thought would do nicely, and the house was just half a mile from the University of Southern California. This was a real plus in Emma's mind. May was finishing high school this year, and Grace was not far behind her. What an excellent opportunity for them to live right next door to a university. They could even walk there and back!

The university had an illustrious history. In the early 1870's, Judge Robert Maclay Widney had a vision of a fine university in the area. In 1879, he formed a board of trustees with three men: Ozro W. Childs, a Protestant horticulturist, John G. Downey, a former governor, an Irish

Catholic pharmacist and business manager. Isaias W. Hellman was a German Jewish banker and philanthropist. This ecumenical group donated 308 lots, and a building was built. In 1880, the university opened with fifty-three students and ten teachers. At the time Los Angeles had no paved streets, electric lights, telephones or fire alarm system.

Emma made an offer on the house, and it was accepted. She moved her family in, and they registered in the nearby schools and things finally started to settle down. Emma commuted to the farm. The wood business was good, the usual barley and alfalfa crops were planted and harvested. The truck garden continued to thrive.

Late that spring, Sarah received a letter from her sister, Katie Reasoner. She would be traveling with her son, Matthew, from Urbana, Illinois out to California and would be visiting them in Los Angeles. Sarah was overjoyed as she had not seen Katie in many years. Emma and the children were excited as they began a flurry of preparations.

Katie and Matthew's visit became a wonderful family reunion. At one point during the visit, Sarah and Katie launched into a conversation in Yiddish, reminiscing about their time with the Jewish families in Fort Wayne.

Grace, with a puzzled look on her face, turned to her mother and whispered, "What in the world language is that?"

"It's Yiddish," Emma replied. "They learned to speak it a long time ago."

May graduated from high school later that year and was and was now a beautiful young woman. She started classes at USC in the fall. The school had grown remarkably and now filled a lovely landscaped campus.

Grace was something of a tomboy and loved to go exploring with her younger brothers. One day her outdoor adventures with her siblings ended for good.

The trio was fascinated with the nearby railroad tracks. They loved to watch the locomotives roar by pulling loaded cars. Near their home was a trestle over a ravine. One day as they approached this structure. Glen shouted, "Let's run across!"

Earl grinned, "Yes, let's!"

Grace hesitated, "What if a train comes?"

"We'll hear it. We can run fast." Glen turned to Grace, "Are you coming or not?"

"Of course," she replied, refusing to let her brothers know how scared she was.

Partway across, the screech of a train whistle split the air. The boys started running for their lives. Grace panicked, and froze.

"Run, run!" the boys shouted at her.

Finally, she started to move. Her legs felt like lead. She dove off the track on the other side just as the train roared through. Her heart was pounding out of her chest, and she had wet her pants.

Her brothers told their mother about Grace's near escape and Emma forbade her to go out with her brothers ever again. "You are too old to be doing things like this, and you are not smart enough to keep yourself out of trouble."

These words cut into Grace's soul and stayed there, becoming a big part of her subsequent feelings of inferiority.

Sadly, May was not able to finish her first year at USC as she started running a series of fevers. Her cheeks would flush, and the fever would peak every afternoon. Emma did not like this at all. After this had gone on for several weeks, Emma called a doctor, and he came by to check on May.

"I believe she has consumption," he said. "I am so sorry. Just keep her quiet and try to get her to eat nourishing food."

May had no appetite. She began losing weight and coughing incessantly. Fear grasped at Emma. She knew people who had recovered from consumption, but most did not. Was she going to lose her beautiful angel child?

Grace was very close to her sister. She picked up on her mother's fear and adopted it as her own. Emma did not want the other children catching the awful disease too, so she kept them out of the sickroom. Grace, however, sneaked in when her mother was away or busy and talked with May. May loved the company but would warn Grace not to come close.

The months dragged by. May was still with them, but barely. She was so thin, she was emaciated. But her beautiful face still shone with hope. The coughing spells came more frequently, and often she coughed up blood. Emma spent hours at night sitting by May's bedside. She thought back to the time she had fallen completely in love with this child. It was because of May that she married her father and bore three more children. This step-daughter had been a real blessing with a gentle nature and a joyful spirit. Emma felt this was the hardest thing she had ever had to do. Letting go hurt so much, but May was suffering. And so it was a bittersweet time when late one night Emma's angel child stopped breathing. "Go in peace, dear child," Emma whispered.

Emma

1903 - 1910

HEMET

MAY WAS BURIED in Rosedale cemetery near her father, Lewis. Emma sunk into a deep depression. Grief seemed to overwhelm her, but she did not let it keep her from what she had to do. She continued to make her trips to the farm, but even that had lost its savor. She was thankful for her mother, as Sarah kept the household going and even though grieving herself, she was there for the children. Sarah noticed that Grace, the closest sibling in age to May had pulled into herself and seemed distant and preoccupied. She mentioned this to Emma, but Emma was overwhelmed emotionally. She told Sarah to let Grace deal with her loss on her own. "She's old enough now, practically a woman herself, to know that life has its trials and losses." And so the three women in the household moved forward, each in her own private misery.

Emma went from day to day, moving by sheer will. She had been planning to sell some of the ranch property for over three years, but getting settled in their new home and May's subsequent illness and death, had put her efforts on hold. Now, she felt that both she and her family needed a change of scenery, away from the place of their terrible loss.

In a very short time, they found a buyer for sixty acres of the property. Emma received a good price as it was excellent farmland.

With the proceeds in the bank, Emma started looking for a new home. She had heard about a developing area in a remote valley nestled under towering mountains, so one day she boarded the train and traveled to the San Jacinto Valley to look over prospects. She was impressed with the wild beauty of the place as she traveled about the area. The looming presence of the San Jacinto Mountains was calming. A thought leapt to her consciousness, *I would love living in this place!*

After several days, she found just what she had been looking for. It was a property called the Maple Leaf Ranch, and it hugged rock covered hills at the west end of the valley. There was a house, but what took Emma's eye was the eucalyptus grove on the edge of the property. She took in the abundance of wood and could see a harvest waiting to happen. She could go into the wood business right here. She certainly knew how that worked. She itched to get a crew and start cutting, selling and then replanting the fast-growing trees. Emma bought the property, then took the train back to Los Angeles to tell her family.

Everyone seemed excited about the prospect of a new adventure except Sarah. "That is a long way from all my activities in my church and the WCTU," she said wistfully.

"Well," Emma replied. There is a Methodist Episcopal Church in the nearby town of Hemet. We will all be getting involved there, I'm sure. Mama, if you feel you need to stay in Los Angeles, I am sure you could live with Ada. She loves you and would be so happy to have you."

Sarah was silent for a moment, then spoke up. "No, I will go with you. You and the children need me more, especially after losing May."

Emma sighed a breath of relief. It was true, she depended a lot on Sarah.

Emma sat back and looked at her mother. *It is strange how you get used to having someone around, and you really don't appreciate them until you might lose their presence,* she thought to herself. She suddenly saw Sarah in an entirely different light. *She looks so old,* she reflected. Sarah, always slight, had hardened to a lean, wiry silhouette. Her skin stretched taut over her high cheekbones. Her face reflected her long, difficult life. Her mouth set in a thin line, she still looked capable of facing any future difficulties. Steel grey hair pulled back in a bun completed the picture. *She is old.* Emma admitted to herself. *And I am not getting any younger either.*

Emma never spent more than a few minutes a day in front of a mirror and that only long enough to fix her hair. Today, she took a good look. Wrinkles were emerging around her eyes from squinting while out in the sun. Her body was still lean enough as she worked hard and had inherited Sarah's build, but her dark hair had many grey streaks in it now. *Well, I may be getting older, but I still have a lot of work to do!*

There was much to accomplish before they could move to the San Jacinto Valley. With sixty acres now sold, Emma set out to find someone to lease the remainder of the property in Compton. At the same time she was looking at lots in the town of Maywood as an investment, so she proceeded with purchasing these. She was becoming an astute negotiator, and could see the area as potential for growth. She resolved that when she had enough money accumulated she would build small California bungalows on each lot and turn them into rentals. Emma firmly believed in looking down the road and planning ahead.

At last, they were ready for the move. With reliable railroad service between Los Angeles and the San Jacinto Valley, it made sense to move the family that way. Their household belongings and furniture were loaded on freight cars, and the family traveled in the passenger car. They hired a wagon to transport the family and their possessions to the ranch. On top of the list of things to be done was to purchase a farm wagon, a buggy and good horses. Emma saw to that in short order, and the family settled in.

Every Saturday, they made a trip to the town of Hemet for groceries and supplies and again on Sunday to church. The local Methodist

Episcopal Church was a thriving one, and they immediately felt a liking for the minister, a Reverend William Pierce.

While Sarah did not have a large WCTU to become involved in, still the one at the church had a number of dedicated members. She also joined the missionary society and made some good friends there. She missed her former activist life, but she noticed how much she was slowing down with age and felt this was about as much as she could handle.

The children attended Sunday school and became active in the Epworth League which met Sunday evenings. They were old enough now to take the buggy into town by themselves.

Grace had attended one year at USC before the move. She loved to read, but the classes had been hard for her, so she did not miss the opportunity to continue.

Emma set about to get the wood selling business up and running, and it proved to be a successful venture.

They had been living in the Maple Leaf for five years when Emma spotted a lovely two-story white house on Mayberry Avenue in the town of Hemet. It had a for sale sign on it. She stopped, walked up the front path, and knocked on the door. The owner answered the door and seeing Emma's interest, volunteered to show her through the house. Living on the remote ranch had been good, but she was ready to move her family into town. As the children had grown older, they had become more involved with their own activities, and transportation back and forth was a strain.

That night at the supper table, Emma got right to the point.

"I just happened to see a house that looked very interesting. I've been thinking that with all of you are so involved with your goings on in town, that you are hardly at home much anymore. What would you think of moving there?'

Grace sat up and said, "Oh Mama, that would be so nice! I would love living in town!"

"Can we go see it?" Earl asked.

"We can at least drive by and have a look," their mother replied.

Once outside, the owner spotted them and asked everyone in for a tour. Sarah gave her approval, and the children were ecstatic. The next day, Emma made an offer and it was accepted. Emma decided to retain the Maple Leaf property, for now, renting the house and keeping the wood business going herself.

The family made their move to Mayberry Avenue, and everyone seemed pleased with the change. Grace was a young woman now, with a sweet, shy disposition. She had a pleasant face with large bright blue eyes, but her outstanding attraction was her magnificent head of dark hair. When she let it down it cascaded to the back of her knees. She met a young man, William Martin, at Epworth League. A shy friendship began which soon turned into courtship.

Will was a handsome Cornishman who farmed a walnut ranch for his mother. James and Mary Martin had emigrated from Cornwall on their honeymoon. James had worked in the Empire Mine in Grass Valley for many years, then in his own mine in Randsburg after that. Suffering from the miner's disease, silicosis, he moved to the San Gabriel Valley and went into farming. Will and his brothers and sister were born there. Like all Cornish miner folk, the Martins were staunch Methodists, so the faith issue was not a problem.

Grace and Will became engaged in early 1910 and began planning a spring wedding. The couple agreed that they wanted a simple home wedding and the Mayberry house was spacious enough to be the perfect place for this event.

The three women in the household began work on Grace's wedding dress. It turned out beautifully, made of ivory crepe de chine with a lace yoke and cuffs. Tiny tucks encircled her small waist.

The wedding was lovely in its simplicity. The Reverend Pierce performed the ceremony, Grace's brother, Glen and Will's cousin Eusebius
Pollard served as witnesses. Since May was gone, Grace did not have an
attendant. She just did not feel that anyone else could fill that spot. Several
friends of the family attended, and Emma and Sarah served dinner to all
the guests. The wedding took place on April 13, 1910.

Emma noticed just how happy Grace seemed. As for herself, she
felt pleased with her current life.

ADA BISBEE, AGE 26

ADA BISBEE IN HER DEACONESS DRESS

SARAH BISBEE IN HER LAST YEARS

ADA BISBEE AND HER NEW HAT

RILEY BISBEE IN HIS LAST YEARS

Ada and Sarah

1911-1914

A Reunion

THE YEAR 1911 was a landmark year for Sarah. The male voters in California approved full women's suffrage. A woman named Clara Elizabeth Chan became the first Chinese American woman voter in the United States. Sarah together with her daughters, Emma and Ada, were ecstatic. Emma and Sarah made the trip to Los Angeles and met Ada for a celebration dinner in a restaurant.

As they lingered over dishes of chocolate mousse and cups of coffee, Sarah sat back and said, "I am seventy-six years old now, an old woman in anybody's book. I have worked for the vote for women almost all my adult life. At times it was so discouraging that I thought it would never happen. I am so glad I have lived long enough to experience this!"

Ada looked at her mother, thinking about how remarkable she was and how much she loved her. "Mama, do you think it is time you came and lived with me now? Emma has had you to herself for long enough, I think." She poked her sister playfully. "You said you stayed with her so long because the children needed you, but they are all grown up now."

Sarah acknowledged that this was true. Grace was married and living with her husband's family on the walnut farm. Glen had moved to

Buttonwillow in the southern part of the San Joaquin Valley. Emma had helped him with a down payment on some farmland there. He met and courted a woman named Victoria Perry, and they were to be married soon. Only Earl was still living at home, but he was an adult and busy with his own life. True, Grace was going through a hard time as her first baby, a little boy named Alfard Dwight, who had died shortly after birth. She could use this as an excuse for staying, but wouldn't there always be something?

It's time, she thought, *I really would love to spend time with Ada.*

Turning to her, Sarah said, "Yes, I think you're right. It is time. I would love to come live with you."

"Wonderful, Mama. I am so glad. Now that I have my beautiful place up in the La Canada hills, I am sure you will be happy there."

Several weeks later, Emma helped her mother move to La Canada and into Ada's home.

Emma and Ada had been the closest of any of the six Bisbee siblings. They had made that early vow to stay single together, but even though Emma went back on her part of the vow and married Lewis Sexton, Ada forgave her. Ada, on the other hand, had never strayed from her commitment.

Early in her life she had dedicated her life to God and asked only to be allowed to serve Him as He saw fit. She had taught for several years while volunteering for different jobs in her church, but one day her minister had asked her if she had ever considered becoming a deaconess in the Methodist Episcopal Church.

Women who served as deaconesses were paid a salary and served the church in many ways: preparing communion, counseling women members, and calling on the sick and elderly. Ada did become a deaconess and was honored in a special dedication service at the church. She wore a special garb, a dark dress and a white hat that set her apart.

"I'm sort of like a Methodist nun," she laughed. She loved her work and served for many years in this capacity.

Sometimes she called on young women living at the Florence Crittenton Home in Los Angeles. This was a home for unwed mothers, where those finding themselves in the unfortunate situation of expecting a child outside of marriage could come to await the birth of their child.

The staff in the home were impressed with Ada's compassion and dedication and offered her a position. Since she had a particular calling in this direction, she accepted, and after some time, she was promoted to matron of the home. She served there for many years, only retiring very recently as she moved into her new home in La Canada. How she would love having her mother move in with her now to keep her company.

Sarah did love this gracious home set in an orange grove. Her favorite time was in the evening, sitting in her rocking chair on the porch and watching the sunset. Often Ada would sit with her, and they would talk of past times and of people long gone. Sarah knew Ada visited her father, Riley, often, but she never asked her about her visits. Ada, nevertheless, would often give a brief report on him. Sarah had little to say about that.

Sarah had noticed a dark spot on the side of her face. At first, she had thought nothing of it, thinking it just another age spot, but it kept getting larger until one day Ada said, "I'm taking you to a doctor about that. I do not like the looks of it." Ada made an appointment, and a few days later they traveled into Los Angeles to see Ada's doctor.

After examining Sarah, the doctor sighed. "I am concerned about this growth. I want you to see a specialist and have some tests done." Sarah thought this was foolishness, but went along with Ada's urging.

The next week, they again traveled to Los Angeles to see the specialist. They had to wait for the test results. Sarah became even more irritated with the delay. Finally, one day, Ada's telephone rang and when she answered, realized it was the specialist's office. The news was bad. The spreading dark spot was a malignant carcinoma. It was too invasive to be removed surgically. Ada was devastated.

That evening as they sat on the porch, Ada told Sarah the bad news. At first, Sarah didn't say anything. Finally, she sighed. "Well, whatever will be will be. I've had to face some hard things in my life. I can do this one as well. What I do worry about is that I will become a burden to you."

"Oh, Mama, Mama, Mama, do not ever think that. I want nothing more than to be here for you."

During the second year of Sarah's stay with her daughter, Ada noticed that Sarah sometimes seemed to be somewhere else. She was having trouble remembering recent events and often was confused. *She's slipping,* Ada realized with dismay, *As if the cancer isn't enough for her to deal with, her wonderful mind is going too.*

The disease was spreading, reaching its ugly tentacles out into the side of Sarah's face. At times the pain was unbearable for her, but at other times it would recede, and she would wander quite happily in the fog of her mind.

One day after returning from a trip to visit her father she became very troubled. She waited until Sarah seemed to be free of pain and clear of mind and sat down beside her. "Mama, I need to talk to you. I have been to see Papa. I do not think he can live on his own anymore. The place is a mess, but that is nothing new. The trouble is he is not eating. He's wasting away. He needs someone to look after him. After all, he's eighty-three now. I want to bring him here to care for him. Mama, I need to know if you are all right with this."

Sarah looked at her daughter. It was clear that she understood the ramifications of this. She took her time answering. "Of course it's all right with me. If he needs you to take care of him, you must do that. I worry that the two of us will be too much for you, though."

"I will be fine," Ada replied. "I just do not want you upset over him being here, on top of everything else you are going through."

"Ada, I do not hate him. I have always cared about what happened to him. I will be fine."

Ada moved Riley into the La Canada house. He had some problems adjusting to the new situation, and he eyed Sarah cautiously. They spoke politely to one another, but Sarah, for her part avoided him. Riley took to sitting in the rocking chair on the porch in the evening, so Sarah went early to her room instead. After a few days of this, Ada dragged another rocking chair out on the porch. Sarah appeared to ignore it. Several more days went by, then one evening, Sarah made her way out on the porch and sat down by Riley.

They rocked in silence for some time. Finally, Riley spoke up. "Sarah, I've been wanting to say some things to you for a long time. I know I treated you badly for years; the children too. I wish I could go back and do those years over. If I could, I would have tried to be good to you. You deserved that much."

Sarah looked sideways at him. "I believe you," she said quietly.

"I stopped drinking a long time ago," Riley continued, "but that wasn't my real problem. It just seemed that when we lost the ranch in the flood, I felt I had lost myself. I didn't think I was a man anymore. I thought I was a failure and I took it out on you and the children. You did not deserve that."

Sarah's mind was clear tonight. "Riley, those years on the Sacramento were some of the happiest in my life. We had to work so hard, but it was good work, and then we had the children. I wish it could have gone on like that forever."

"Yes, it was good, very good," Riley replied.

"Remember, Riley, our first wedding anniversary? You brought me a bouquet of wild-flowers?"

"I remember," Riley murmured. He reached out and took Sarah's hand. She did not pull it away. The next day, Riley hobbled out into a nearby field and picked a bouquet of lupine and poppies. Bringing it onto the porch that evening, he handed it to Sarah. "Here's another anniversary bouquet, even if it isn't an anniversary. You deserved many of these, dear girl."

Riley and Sarah sat each evening rocking on the porch. Sometimes they talked quietly, sometimes they just rocked in companionable silence. Riley knew Sarah was dying. He also accepted that he might not be around much longer. He wondered which one of them would go first. As it turned out Riley was. Getting up one morning, he collapsed to the floor. By the time the doctor arrived, he was gone.

"Apoplexy," the doctor intoned. "A stroke."

Ada notified her brothers and sisters, and a few days later, they arrived to attend his burial in Rosedale cemetery. Sarah was there too, though in very bad shape. She managed her goodbyes in private.

Sarah's condition worsened rapidly, but she lived for another year after Riley died. It was a difficult time for Ada as she saw her mother suffering so much. By the end, Sarah's mind was gone. When she wasn't in pain, she thought she was back in the cabin in the Indiana woods with her mother and her sisters. It was with a feeling of great relief that when she went to Sarah's room early one morning, she saw she was no longer breathing.

"Thank you Lord for taking her home," she sighed with tears running down her face.

EMMA SEXTON IN HER LATER YEARS

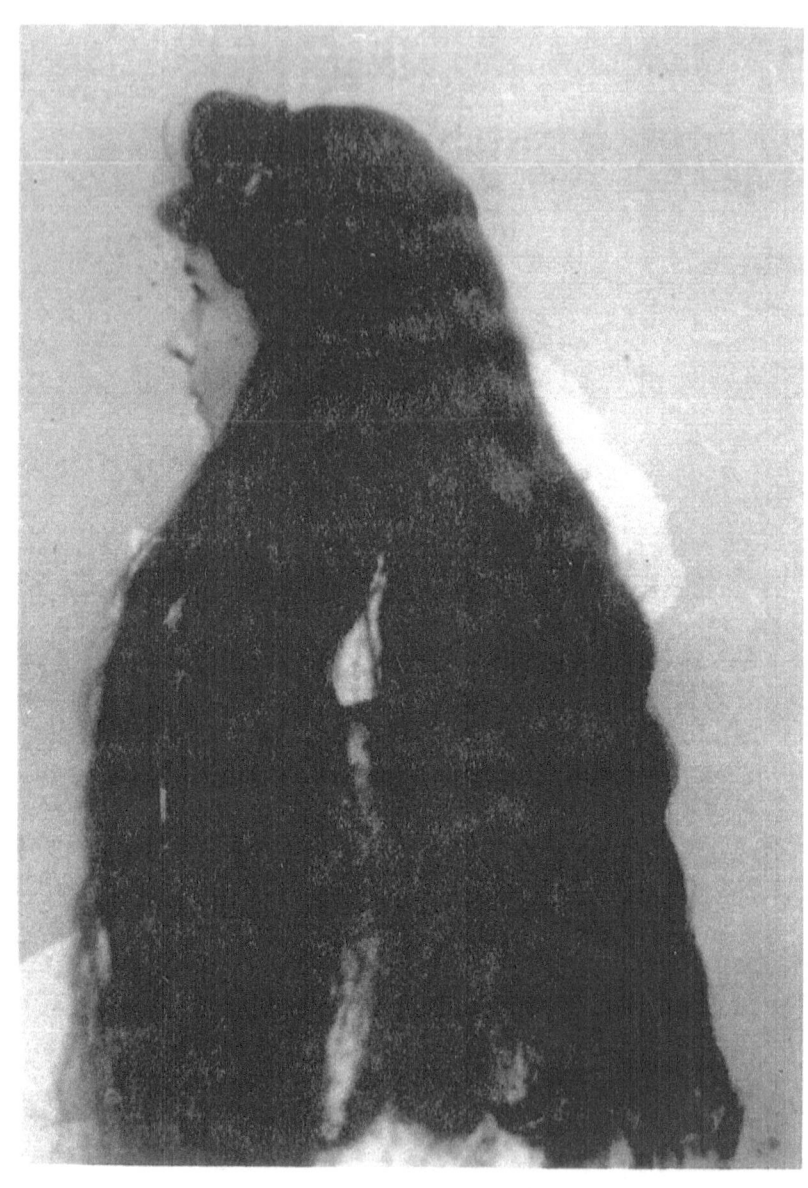

GRACE AND HER BEAUTIFUL HAIR

GRACE SEXTON AND WILLIAM MARTIN
ON THEIR WEDDING DAY, HEMET, CALIFORNIA
APRIL 13, 1910

WILL AND GRACE MARTIN
WITH THEIR CHILDREN, HAROLD AND ADA DOROTHY

$\mathcal{E}$mma

1914 - 1923

OIL WELLS

SARAH'S DEATH WAS bittersweet, Emma thought. She was thankful that her mother's suffering was over, but she missed her terribly, as did Ada. As usual, Emma's remedy for grief was to keep busy.

She had became a grandmother twice over the year before: Glen's wife, Victoria had a little boy, Louis, and Grace having recovered from her loss of two years before, gave birth to a healthy son, Harold Richard.

Emma made the trip up to Buttonwillow to see Glen and Victoria's baby but knew further trips would be few and far between; it was just too far and she was busy. Grace, still lived in the valley and she saw her and the baby often.

While Emma prided herself on her business acumen and ability to function in a man's world, she knew she had a softer side, and that was the one that adored children. She rejoiced in her role as grandmother.

Her son, Earl, stayed with her until America entered World War I on April 6, 1917. Earl joined the army shortly after that and was shipped to England where he was stationed during the duration of the war.

Earl met a young English woman, Evelyn, and they were married. Emma received the news with a stoic attitude. She did not think a wartime marriage was wise, but Earl was a grown man now. When he wrote that Evelyn was expecting a baby, Emma melted. She could not resist the appeal of another grandchild. Sadly, this was not to be. Medical care was not what it should have been in wartime England. Evelyn suffered from Bright's disease, resulting in eclampsia. Both she and the baby died. Even though Emma had never met her daughter-in-law, she felt a sharp sense of loss. She knew her son must be devastated, but all she could do was write him letters of encouragement. The war ended. Earl came home along with many other American servicemen, and the country seemed to prosper.

Grace now had a baby daughter, Ada Dorothy. Emma was overjoyed. She had encouraged Grace to name the baby after her Aunt Ada if it was a girl. Relishing the role of grandmother, Emma spent many hours with the small boy and girl.

Grace and Will now had their own home, built on Hemet's main street, Florida Avenue. Emma had been pleased with her daughter demanding a home of her own. She sometimes worried that Grace was too sweet and compliant, but had changed her mind over the house issue.

After a short time living in the Mayberry house, Will and Grace had moved into Will's mother's home east of town. His father had succumbed to silicosis a few years before, but Will's brothers also lived there. Will felt that it was a practical decision as he was farming the land for his mother. However, Grace was miserable. Her mother-in-law was a strong woman who ran her home with an iron hand. Grace was treated like a second-class resident, and she hated it. Finally, she told her husband that he had to find a place of their own to live, or she would leave. Emma backed her up on this and it worked. A new home was built for the little family.

Emma still owned the Maple Leaf, the remaining farmland in Compton, as well as rentals and lots in Maywood. She ran a successful wood business from the Maple Leaf. In the years after World War I, something unusual was taking place in the Los Angeles basin. It had its beginnings many years before in 1892 when two men became partners.

Edward Doheny and Charles Canfield drilled an oil well, and a remarkable era began. Oil seeps had been evident for years in the area, not only in the Los Angeles basin but into Orange and Ventura Counties. One notable example was the La Brea Tar Pits.

After the first well, oil fields sprang up all over, spreading into Beverly Hills and reaching to Montbello and Santa Fe Springs. A push was on to move from the use of coal to fuel oil and gasoline. The advent and popularity of the automobile increased the demand. The craze reached out and touched Emma Sexton in 1919 when the two men traveled on the Santa Fe railway from Los Angeles to Hemet.

Dressed in proper suits and ties, they made their way by foot the few blocks from the railway station to the house on Mayberry Avenue and knocked on Emma's door. If Emma was surprised to see two well-dressed strangers standing on her porch, she did not show it. After ascertaining that they indeed had arrived at the right house, they introduced themselves as land men for an oil company. Emma invited them in. They seated themselves in her parlor.

Her curiosity got the better of her, and she did not offer them any refreshment, but instead asked, "What do you want with me?"

"You are the owner of some land in Compton?" the copper-haired one asked.

"Yes," she replied, "Why?'

"Our company would like to put some oil wells on that land."

The short, fat man interjected, "Yours is prime property for oil, ma'am."

Emma's heart was beating wildly, but she did not show her excitement. "Is it indeed?" she replied coolly.

Emma had many, many questions for the landmen and they were obviously amazed at her business acumen. After going over the contract in detail, they reached an agreement. As the men departed to catch the late afternoon train back to Los Angeles, Emma realized that she was now in the oil business.

She decided that it was time to sell the Maple Leaf and get out of the wood business. People were not buying wood in the amount used in the past. Even so, in 1919 when she sold her last load, she was paid almost double the amount per cord as when she first started. Her Mexican crew was sad to see the business closed, but she promised them a good reference to the new owners.

As the wells went in on the Compton property, Emma found herself caught up in the process. She made frequent trips to see the progress being made. The southern Los Angeles basin was experiencing a frenzy of activity. Wildcat wells were springing up everywhere. A forest of wooden derricks dotted former farmlands. The hypnotic up and down movement of the walking beams denoted the constant pursuit of the black gold.

On one of her trips to Compton, Emma noted that the walking beams on two of the wells were motionless. When she inquired of the foreman why this was, he explained that the heavy tool bit that dug into the earth had broken in both units. The rock and rubble en-countered by the three to five-ton tool bit sometimes blocked and broke loose from its cable. He further told her that they would have to use what he called a fishing tool to go down in the well to retrieve the tool bit.

About two weeks later, she asked Will and Grace if they would like to take a trip to the Los Angeles area and look at the wells. Will expressed an interest in this and one day, they set out with the children and adults all packed into Will's Ford together with a picnic lunch. Upon driving up to the oil field, Emma was dismayed to see that the two wells were still not in service. She knew that sometimes the tool bit could be so severely wedged in the drill hole, that the only recourse would be to drill new wells. But there was no sign of that either.

Emma exploded from the Ford and marched up to the foreman she had spoken to two weeks ago. "What is the meaning of this? Why aren't these wells in service, or why haven't new wells been drilled if the tool bits cannot be retrieved?"

The tall man, unshaven and covered in oil drew himself up and looked down at her with contempt, "For God's sake lady, we've been busy here, can't you see? We'll get around to it!"

Emma could not believe his arrogant lackadaisical attitude. She received a percentage of the production as income, and these idle wells were not producing. Emma was getting older, but she was still a force to be reckoned with. Her straight back and determined carriage were even more imposing now. With her clear unwrinkled skin and abundant grey hair pulled up in a bun, she was a striking woman.

"What are you thinking of?" she shouted at the foreman. "Get these wells in production immediately or start drilling some replacements!"

The foreman sneered at her, "I don't take orders from no woman!" he spat.

Emma did not hesitate. She picked up a shovel lying on the ground and started after the foreman with it raised over her head. "You will do what I say, or you will regret it!" she said in a calm determined voice that was much more frightening than a shout.

"All right, all right, settle down, lady, we'll get right at it."

"Just see that you do."

Emma put the shovel down and returned to the car. Her grandson, Harold, was awestruck at this powerful, angry woman that was his grandmother. He would remember the scene for the rest of his life.

In 1922, a tank farm company offered to buy forty acres of the Compton property for $40,000. With this windfall, Emma was able to buy up more real estate both in the Los Angeles area and in San Bernardino County. She built small California bungalows on many of the lots and sold these, investing in more as she went along. She loved the real estate business, and she was acquiring some substantial wealth. This allowed her to help out her children when the need arose. At times, she would reflect on her life and acknowledge that she had been able to turn adversity around. Rather than let trials and loss defeat her, she had thrived and triumphed.

Emma

1931

ARRIVAL OF THE AFTERTHOUGHT

EMMA SAT AT her kitchen table, a cooling cup of tea in front of her as she took stock of her life. She loved this place, a Craftsman-style home in Yucaipa, which she bought in 1927. She did not need the big house in Hemet anymore as she seemed to rattle around in its two stories like a single marble in a maze.

She found the Yucaipa home during her real estate dealings and fell in love with it. It suited her just fine. She planted an extensive cactus garden and several fruit trees which did not require the attention that a more formal garden needed. She brought in someone to prune the fruit trees in winter and pick the fruit in the summer. Her arthritis was a constant reminder that she could not do the heavy work she used to. After all, she was almost an octogenarian, so slowing down was part of the process even though she fought it all the way. The last few years were not easy.

Looking back, she thought of 1924 when everything seemed to be going her way. She invested wisely and well. She succeeded in a career that was almost exclusively occupied by men. The oil wells produced admirably. 1919 and 1920 saw the Compton oil field thoroughly into production. It was only part of a much larger phenomenon.

Signal Hill in Long Beach had exploded due to the tenacity of two men, geologists with Shell Oil: Frank Hayes, and Alvin Theodore Schwennesen. Work began on the Alamitos #1 well on March 23rd, 1921. By May 2nd, 70 feet of standing oil was found at the bottom of the hole. Nothing further happened until June 23rd when at 9:30 PM the Alamitos #1 erupted with so great a gas pressure that oil gushed 114 feet into the air. Unfortunately, the bottom of the hole caved in, and much work was required to clean it up, but by June 25, 1921, the well was producing 1,000 barrels a day. The well would eventually produce 700,000 barrels of oil.

The rush was on. The discovery started a stampede. The Signal Hill area was in the process of being subdivided into residential lots. Many of the lots, while already sold, were not yet built upon and potential homeowners quickly changed their minds and started looking for oil, hoping to get rich quick. The parcels of land were so small, and the forest of tall wooden derricks so thick, that the legs of many of them actually intertwined. The next-of-kin of persons buried in the Sunnyside Cemetery of Willow Street would eventually receive royalty checks for oil drawn out from beneath family grave plots.

Signal Hill was the largest field the already productive southern California region had ever seen. In 1923, Signal Hill produced 244,000 barrels, alongside Huntington Beach (discovered in 1920) at 113,000 and Santa Fe (1921) at 32,000. This made California the number one oil-producing state, and in 1923, California was the source of one-quarter of the world's entire output of oil!

As Emma thought about the unexpected discovery of oil on her inherited property, she smiled to herself. Of course, Lewis Sexton had no idea of this when he bought the rich farmland so many years ago. Emma laughed out loud. What was even more of a twist was that Ada had sold her home in La Canada and bought a lot in Huntington Beach. She did so love being near the ocean. Her lot ended up being smack in the middle of the Huntington Beach Bolsa Chica Field! Indeed she and her sister had been blessed beyond their wildest dreams.

Ah well…things had not gone so well lately. The financial crash of 1929 had left the country in the middle of the Great Depression. Many of Emma's properties came back to her. Emma did not let this setback get her down. She saw it as just another challenge. So, the money was not coming in as before, and there was the expense of foreclosures and repairs. She just put her frugal management hat on and went through her difficulties, knowing that the bad times could not last forever.

This morning she was in a reflective mood. She thought back over her life. After all, someone about to turn eighty should have that prerogative. She thought of her losses. Those lying under the green lawns of Rosedale Cemetery in downtown Los Angeles: Lewis her husband of eight years, her beloved stepdaughter, May, her parents, Sarah and Riley. One day she would be placed next to Lewis, she knew. She grieved over those lost, even the little grandson in the San Jacinto Valley Cemetery and the little one and his mother buried somewhere in England.

Losses were hard, but she thought, *At least I had some of these to love for a time. My darling angel child, May, and her father who I came to love and gone too soon. My parents, especially that remarkable woman, my mother, Sarah. I have been rich indeed! And I have my remaining children and my grandchildren. I have been truly blessed.*

She chuckled to herself as she thought back to the New Year of this year, 1931. Will and Grace had driven from Hemet to Yucaipa as they often did, but this time, Grace had some news.

Will had gone outside to look over her fruit trees, and she and Grace were alone when Grace said, "Mama, I'm going to have another baby, sometime next summer."

Emma gasped, "For heavens' sake, Grace, you are forty-five years old! That's much too old to be having another baby!"

Grace had expected this outburst. She knew her mother well, and Emma had never been one to withhold an opinion.

"Well," Grace replied. "We didn't exactly plan for this, it just happened."

Emma huffed a dramatic sigh of exasperation, "And what are you going to tell this child–that he or she was an accident?"

"No, mama," Grace spoke in a calm, quiet voice. "I will my sweet child that he or she was an afterthought."

"Well, I never!" Emma gasped.

Emma knew her bark was worse than her bite. She was not sure that Grace understood that. Secretly she was pleased as punch that a new grand-baby was on the way. She was also pleased that Grace had stood up to her as she had. *She could show some spunk when she wanted to,* Emma acknowledged. She allowed herself a moment's pang as she thought that maybe she had given Grace too little praise over the years.

Well, well, well, another baby, Emma surmised, *Harold at seventeen and Dorothy at fifteen would spoil the baby rotten, but she would get her licks in too.*

Emma got up slowly from her seat by the kitchen window. She took her cup and saucer to the sink and washed them under the tap, putting them on a tea towel to dry. She noticed that it was beginning to get hot in the house. It was to be expected on a summer day. The telephone started to ring. Emma's arthritis slowed her down. She just hoped she could get to the phone before the person hung up. It was still ringing when she reached for it. "Hello," she said, toughening her voice so she would not sound as weak as she felt.

"Mama?" Grace's voice came over the line.

Emma had kept her worry about Grace having a baby at her advanced age to herself, but suddenly the fear overwhelmed her, "Are you all right?"

"Oh yes, mama. I am fine. Sore, but fine. I had a baby girl this morning. She's big, and she's healthy. She is a beautiful baby."

Emma let out a sigh of relief, "Oh my, do you know what day this is?"

"I surely do, mama. It's the fourth of July!"

Emma couldn't help herself, "A little firecracker is she?"

Grace was amazed at her mother's jolly teasing that was so unlike her. "That's right. She will think all the fireworks are to celebrate her birthday. We are naming her Anita Louise."

"That's a good name, Grace. I can't wait to meet her. Please bring her to see me as soon as you are strong enough."

"I'll do that, mama."

Emma hung up the phone. She felt like singing and dancing. She couldn't manage the dancing on arthritic legs, but she could surely sing, After all, there wasn't anyone around to hear her making a fool of herself.

THE AFTERTHOUGHT
ANITA LOUISE MARTIN, AGE 18 MONTHS

1936

ANITA LOUISE MARTIN

I AM FIVE years old and today is a good day. I sit in the back seat of my daddy's Ford. My big brother, Harold, is driving and my mama is sitting beside him. We are traveling to my grandma's house in Yucaipa for a visit. We visit often, but I get excited about each trip. We have to travel from Hemet, past San Jacinto then up over the rocky hills on a very windy road called the Jackrabbit Trail. It comes out near the town of Beaumont. Then it is just a little further to grandma's house in Yucaipa.

My daddy used to drive us over here a lot, but my grandma and daddy don't get along so good any more. My mama tells me it was a big misunderstanding, but since it was about me, I can't help but want to know all about it.

I guess it happened a long time ago when I was about two or maybe three. Sometimes I was a very naughty girl. Anyway, one day at grandma's I was sitting on my daddy's lap when I did this terrible thing—I spat at him. Daddy just put up his hand and caught my spit and rubbed it in my face. I screamed bloody murder and grandma thought he hit me. My daddy never hit me, but I sure deserved having my face rubbed with spit. I never did spit again.

The problem was my grandma would not believe that he did not hit me. So now daddy stays home. He had a lot of work to do anyway down at Martin's Hemet Theater where he is the boss, and I get to see free movies and cartoons.

As we travel along, I think about the last time I visited grandma. She has this beautiful cactus garden with all kinds of strange and different cactus growing in it. There was one that had all this furry stuff covering it. It looked just like a fluffy animal. I had to pet it, but it bit me! I ran screaming into the house with all these stickers in my hand. Grandma pulled them out. Boy, did it hurt! But she put some kind of cream on my hand, and it felt better. This time, I would be sure not to touch any of that cactus.

At last, we're here. We knock on the door, and Uncle Earl lets us in. Uncle Earl lives with grandma and takes care of her because she is in a wheelchair and can't do a lot of things for herself. Mama says she has bad arthritis, that's why she has to be in the wheelchair. Right when I come in the door, grandma wheels her chair into the room and says, "Where's my favorite little girl?"

"I'm here, grandma," I answer, and she leans over and gives me a big hug.

Grandma has on a dark dress and black lace-up shoes that peek out under the blanket covering her lap. She has this strong face and a cloud of white hair around her head. Her hands are twisted, but that does not stop her from wheeling up to the kitchen table and reaching for the bread. She slices off a piece and puts some strawberry jam on it. As she hands it to me, she says, "Here's something sweet for a sweet girl."

I wander off and eat my bread and jam as grandma, mama and Harold have a visit. I visit the cactus garden, careful not to touch anything. Then as I come back inside, I hear my grandma's voice. "I found a sticky doorknob! I found a sticky doorknob!" Oh boy, am I ever in trouble now!

She wheels her chair up to me, grabs my hands, and washes them with a cloth. "There, that's better," she says.

I think that my grandma knows everything and sees everything.

After the grownups get through visiting, we say goodbye and leave for home. I am really tired, and as I drift off to sleep I hear my mama tell my brother, "She looks a lot more frail than the last time, but after all, she's well into her eighties now."

Harold says back, "I don't know. She seems to be the same fireball as ever.

I do not hear anymore and sleep until we drive into our driveway and mama wakes me up to go into the house.

The next afternoon, I come in from playing outside and see my mama sitting on the daybed under the dining room windows. She likes to sit there to do her knitting or crocheting or whatever thing she's working on because she can spread it out around her. She reads to me sometimes there, and I curl up beside her. She has already taught me to read, and I'm not even in kindergarten yet. Today, I curl up beside her. "Mama?"

Mama looks down at me. "What is it, dear?"

I think before I go on, then blurt it out, "Grandma's kind of scary isn't she?"

Mama laughs, "She can sometimes be. Just remember though, she thinks the world of you."

I think this over. "Does she really?"

"Oh yes, she loves you very much."

I think some more

OK, I guess I love her too."

Mama keeps on crocheting for a while. She is making a bedspread for me. Then she puts it down and turns to me. "You know, Anita, you have some strong, brave women who came before you. Your grandma is just one of them."

This is something new to me. "Tell me about them, Mama!"

"Well now, there was your great grandma, Sarah. She was grandma's mama, you know. She grew up in a log cabin in the Indiana woods and one night when she was only a little older than you, a big bunch of wolves came up to the cabin and jumped up and looked in the window at them."

Now I sense that this is something important. "Wasn't she scared?"

Mama gives me a hug. "Oh yes, she was scared, but her mama, Mary, wasn't. She went to the fireplace and lit a piece of wood. When it was burning good, she opened the door and threw the burning wood right into the middle of that pack of wolves, and they all ran away!"

I think about little Sarah who was grandma's mama, and grandma is mama's mama, and here I am.

"Tell me more, Mama," I beg.

Acknowledgments

My heartfelt thanks to:

My niece, Julie Martin Burgard, whose quest into the genealogy of our family was the beginning of it all.

My generous cousin, Jim Bisbee, for all the photos and oral histories.

My dedicated first readers, my good friend, the Rev. Dr. Sally Smith and my daughter, Denise Stensrud. Plus all the input from my Inklings writing group.

The helpful staff members at The California State Historical Library in Sacramento, The California Genealogical Society in Oakland, The San Francisco Public Library, The Santa Barbara Historical Society and the Goleta Historical Society.

My third cousin, Colonel Matthew Reasoner, who in 1924 had the foresight to sit down with three elderly ladies, his mother, Katherine Malone Reasoner, his cousins Carrie Bisbee Ledford and Ada Bisbee, and record their oral histories for posterity.

My second cousin, Horace Sexton, who faithfully recorded the history of the other great-grands.

My friend, Dave Iserman, for his pen and ink renderings from the only known photographs of Ann Claypoole Sexton and Richard Sexton.

And especially for my late husband, Norm, for his incredible love and support and for being an outstanding researcher.

Bibliography

1. *To California by Sea*
   James P. Delgado
   University of South Carolina Press, 1990

2. *Sea Routes to the Gold Fields*
   Oscar Lewis
   Alfred Knopf, 1949

3. *James Claypoole's Letter Book*
   London and Philadelphia
   168 –1684
   Ed. Marion Balderston
   The Huntington Library, 1967

4. *Charles Emery Bisbey:*
   An Oral History and Genealogy
   Sharyn Eileen (Bisbey) Fuller

5. *This Was San Francisco - Being First Hand Accounts*
   of the Evolution of One of America's Favorite Cities
   Compiled and edited by Oscar Lewis
   David McKay Co. Inc., New York, 1962

6. *Old San Francisco - The Biography of a City*
   From Early Days to the Earthquake
   David Muscatine
   G.T. Putnam Sons, New York, 1975

7. *Gold Rush Chronology*
   1853 – 4, #3

8. *Yiddish English Dictionary*
   Copyright © 1994-2010
   Thomas A. Gil

9. *Fourteen at the Table*
   An Informal History of the Life and Good Times
   of the Sexton Family of Old Goleta
   Walker A. Tompkins in collaboration with Horace Sexton
   Goleta Valley Historical Society, 1988

About the Author

Anita Martin-Harvey is the great-granddaughter and granddaughter of the women in *Legacy*. She is a third generation California.

While married to her first husband, a minister, she raised ten children, five by birth and five by adoption from Korea. After the children were grown, she returned to school, finished her undergraduate degree and earned a Masters in Counseling Psychology from Gonzaga University in Spokane, Washington.

As a single person she moved to the San Francisco Bay area and had a career in vocational rehabilitation counseling and was a rehabilitation coordinator for a large corporation.

She retired in 2000 and married the love of her life, Norman Harvey. They moved to the foothills of the Sierra. She lost Norm in 2013, but continues to live in Sonora where she enjoys reading, writing and many creative activities with her friends.

www.ingramcontent.com/pod-product-compliance
Lightning Source LLC
Chambersburg PA
CBHW031116030726
47496CB00002BA/576